Virginia Driving Hawk Sneve

Grandpa Was

a Cowboy

& an Indian

and Other Stories

University of Nebraska Press

Lincoln & London

Acknowledgments for the use of
previously published material
appear on page 115,
which constitutes an extension
of the copyright page.

∞

First Nebraska paperback printing: 2003
Library of Congress Cataloging-in-Publication Data
Sneve, Virginia Driving Hawk
Grandpa was a cowboy and an Indian and other stories /
Virginia Driving Hawk Sneve.
p.   cm.
ISBN 0-8032-4274-3 (cloth: alk. paper)
ISBN 0-8032-9300-3 (paper: alk. paper)
1. Indians of North America—Social life and customs—Fiction.
I. Title.
PS3569.N474 G73 2000
813'.54—dc21   00-023483

Contents

Author's Note

I grew up on the Rosebud Sioux Indian Reservation in South Dakota. I was surrounded by a loving extended family of many relatives. Most important among them, besides my mother and father, were my grandparents.

In my childhood, many of the societal customs of the Lakota and Dakota had not changed, so I spent most of my time with my grandmothers, from whom I learned how to be a good woman. They did not lecture; they taught by precept and example. As part of the latter, they told stories. My maternal grandmother, Harriet Ross, and her mother, Hannah Frazier, told of the Dakota experience in history and in legend. My Lakota grandmother on my father's side, Flora Driving Hawk, also told legends. She was such a skilled oral storyteller that I longed to emulate her in written words.

I was also fortunate in knowing my grandfathers, Edward Ross and Robert Driving Hawk, and my great-grandfather, Charles

Frazier. From them I learned how life had been for brave and fearless warriors and how these displaced men adapted to a passive reservation life. Their first care was their families, and they worked at many tasks in order to provide economic support for their loved ones.

Charles, a Santee Dakota, was an infant when the Santee were exiled from Minnesota after the 1862 uprising. He became an ordained minister of the Congregational Church, but he also farmed. Edward and Robert, both Lakota, had worked as cowboys in their youth. Both became ranchers after their marriages and kept at that until drought and low cattle prices forced them to other occupations. But they never lost their love for horses and the life those magnificent creatures represented.

Over the years, my grandfathers' individual experiences mingled with the tales of my grandmothers to become part of my novels. The novels *Jimmy Yellow Hawk* and *Betrayed* have been long out of print, but to my amazement, teachers (especially from reservation schools) find the books and often ask where they can be purchased. In this collection, I have included the original short-story versions of those novels.

Other stories became short fiction, nonfiction, and legends and were published in reading texts or literature anthologies for use in school classrooms. These had a limited readership.

All of the characters in the stories (save the Fool Soldiers) are fictional but were often inspired by actual persons and events. The "Fool Soldiers" is based on historic occurrences of the 1862 Minnesota Sioux uprising, which I learned about from my Santee grandparents.

Many of my shorter works are included here along with legends I have written over the years but never published. Legends were told to teach a lesson as well as to entertain children and adults. They showed the importance of proper behavior or explained the beginnings of plants and animals and indeed of all creation. Many tell of the supernatural and the mysteries of life, but they all always contain elements of truth. Those retold here are my personal favorites.

Grandparents told these stories to *Takoža* (grandchild), a representative of all Native American children—every tribe's most treasured possession.

Virginia Driving Hawk Sneve

One

Generations

The Medicine Bag

Grandpa wasn't tall and stately like TV Indians. His hair wasn't in braids; it hung in stringy, gray strands on his neck, and he was old. He was my great-grandfather, and he didn't live in a tipi; he lived all by himself in a part log, part tar-paper shack on the Rosebud Reservation in South Dakota.

My kid sister, Cheryl, and I always bragged about our Lakota grandpa, Joe Iron Shell. Our friends, who had always lived in the city and only knew about Indians from movies and TV, were impressed by our stories. Maybe we exaggerated and made Grandpa and the reservation sound glamorous, but when we returned home to Iowa after our yearly summer visit to Grandpa, we always had some exciting tale to tell.

We usually had some authentic Lakota article to show our listeners. One year Cheryl had new moccasins that Grandpa had made. On another visit he gave me a small, round, flat rawhide drum decorated with a painting of a warrior riding a horse. He taught me a Lakota chant to sing while I beat the drum with a leather-covered stick that had a feather on the end. Man, that really made an impression.

We never showed our friends Grandpa's picture. Not that we were ashamed of him but because we knew that the glamorous tales we told didn't go with the real thing. Our friends would have laughed, so when Grandpa came to visit us, I was so ashamed and embarrassed I could have died.

There are a lot of yippy poodles and other fancy little dogs in our neighborhood, but they usually barked singly at the mailman from the safety of their own yards. Now it sounded as if a whole pack of mutts were barking together in one place.

I walked to the curb to see what the commotion was. About a block away I saw a crowd of little kids yelling, with the dogs yipping and growling around someone who was walking down the middle of the street.

I watched the group as it slowly came closer and saw that in the center of the strange procession was a man wearing a tall black hat. He'd pause now and then to peer at something in his hand and then at the houses on either side of the street. I felt cold and hot at the same time. I recognized the man. "Oh, no!" I whispered, "It's Grandpa!"

I stood on the curb, unable to move even though I wanted to run and hide. Then I got mad when I saw how the yippy dogs were growling and nipping at the old man's baggy pant legs and how wearily he poked them away with his cane. "Stupid mutts," I said as I ran to rescue Grandpa.

When I kicked and hollered at the dogs to get away, they put their tails between their legs and scattered. The kids ran to the curb where they watched me and the old man.

"Grandpa," I said and reached for his beat-up old tin suitcase tied shut with a rope. But he set it down right in the street and shook my hand.

"*Hau, Takoža,* Grandchild," he greeted me formally in Lakota.

All I could do was stand there with the whole neighborhood watching and shake the hand of the leather-brown old man. I saw how his gray hair straggled from under his big black hat, which had a drooping feather in its crown. His rumpled black suit hung like a sack over his stooped frame. As he shook my hand, his coat fell open to expose a bright red satin shirt with a beaded bolo tie under the collar. His getup wasn't out of place on the reservation, but it sure was here, and I wanted to sink right through the pavement.

"Hi," I muttered with my head down. I tried to pull my hand away when I felt his bony hand trembling and then looked up to see fatigue in his face. I felt like crying. I couldn't think of anything to say so I picked up Grandpa's suitcase, took his arm, and guided him up the driveway to our house.

Mom was standing on the steps. I don't know how long she'd been watching, but her hand was over her mouth and she looked as if she couldn't believe what she saw. Then she ran to us.

"Grandpa," she gasped. "How in the world did you get here?"

She checked her move to embrace Grandpa, and I remembered that such a display of affection is unseemly to the Lakota and would have embarrassed him.

"*Hau,* Marie," he said as he shook Mom's hand. She smiled and took his other arm.

As we supported him up the steps, the door banged open and Cheryl came bursting out of the house. She was all smiles and was so obviously glad to see Grandpa that I was ashamed of how I felt.

"Grandpa!" she yelled happily, "You came to see us!"

Grandpa smiled, and Mom and I let go of him as he stretched out his arms to my ten-year-old sister, who was still young enough to be hugged.

"*Wincincila,* little girl," he greeted her and then collapsed.

He had fainted. Mom and I carried him into her sewing room, where we had a spare bed.

After we had Grandpa on the bed, Mom stood there patting his shoulder. "You make Grandpa comfortable, Martin," she decided, "while I call the doctor."

I reluctantly moved to the bed. I knew Grandpa wouldn't want to have Mom undress him, but I didn't want to either. He was so skinny and frail that his coat slipped off easily. When I loosened his tie and opened his shirt collar, I felt a small leather pouch that hung from a thong around his neck. I left it alone and moved to remove his boots. The scuffed old cowboy boots were tight, and he moaned as I put pressure on his legs to jerk them off.

I put the boots on the floor and saw why they fit so tight. Each one was stuffed with money. I looked at the bills that lined the boots and started to ask about them, but Grandpa's eyes were closed again.

Mom came back with a basin of water. "The doctor thinks Grandpa may be suffering from heat exhaustion," she explained as she bathed Grandpa's face. Mom gave a big sigh, "Oh *hinh,* Martin. How do you suppose he got here?"

We found out after the doctor's visit. Grandpa was angrily sitting up in bed while Mom tried to feed him some soup.

"Tonight you let Marie feed you, Grandpa," said my dad, who had gotten home from work. "You're not really sick," he said as he gently pushed Grandpa back against the pillows. The doctor thinks you just got too tired and hot after your long trip."

Grandpa relaxed, and between sips of soup, he told us of his journey. Soon after we visited him, Grandpa decided that he would like to see where his only living descendents lived and what our home was like. Besides, he admitted sheepishly, he was lonesome after we left.

I knew that everybody felt as guilty as I did—especially Mom. Mom was all Grandpa had left. So even after she married my dad, who's not an Indian, and after Cheryl and I were born, Mom made sure that every summer we spent a week with Grandpa.

I never thought that Grandpa would be lonely after our visits, and none of us noticed how old and weak he had become. But Grandpa knew, so he came to us. He had ridden on buses for two and a half days. When he arrived in the city, tired and stiff from sitting for so long, he set out walking to find us.

He had stopped to rest on the steps of some building downtown, and a policeman found him. The officer took Grandpa to the city bus top, waited until the bus came, and then told the driver to let Grandpa out at Bell View Drive. After Grandpa got off the bus, he started walking again. But he couldn't see the house numbers on the other side when he walked on the sidewalk, so he walked in the middle of the street. That's when all the little kids and dogs followed him.

I knew everybody felt as bad as I did. Yet I was so proud of this eighty-six-year-old man who had never been away from the reservation but who had the courage to travel so far alone.

"You found the money in my boots?" he asked Mom.

"Martin did," she answered and then scolded, "Grandpa, you shouldn't have carried so much money. What if someone had stolen it from you?"

Grandpa laughed. "I would've known if anyone tried to take the boots off my feet. The money is what I've saved for a long time—a hundred dollars—for my funeral. But you take it now to buy groceries so that I won't be a burden to you while I am here."

"That won't be necessary, Grandpa," Dad said, "We are honored to have you with us, and you will never be a burden. I am only sorry that we never thought to bring you home with us this summer and spare you the discomfort of a long bus trip."

Grandpa was pleased. "Thank you," he answered. "But don't feel bad that you didn't bring me with you, for I would not have come then. It was not time." He said this in such a way that no one could argue with him. To Grandpa and the Lakota, he once told me, a thing would be done when it was the right time to do it, and that's the way it was.

"Also," Grandpa went on, looking at me. "I have come because it is soon time for Martin to have the medicine bag."

We all knew what that meant. Grandpa thought he was going to die, and he had to follow the tradition of his family to pass the medicine bag, along with its history, to the oldest male child.

"Even though the boy," he said, still looking at me, "doesn't have an Indian name, the medicine bag will be his."

I didn't know what to say. I had the same hot and cold feeling that I had when I first saw Grandpa in the street. The medicine bag was the dirty leather pouch I had found around his neck. "I could never wear it," I almost said aloud. I thought of having my friends see it in gym class or at the swimming pool and could imagine the smart things they would say. But I just swallowed hard and took a step toward the bed. I knew I would have to take it.

But Grandpa was tired. "Not now, Martin," he said waving his hand in dismissal. "It is not time. Now I will sleep."

So that's how Grandpa came to be with us for two months. My friends kept asking to come see the old man, but I put them off.

I told myself that I didn't want them laughing at Grandpa. But even as I made excuses, I knew it wasn't Grandpa I was afraid they'd laugh at.

Nothing bothered Cheryl about bringing her friends to see Grandpa. Every day after school started, there'd be a crew of giggling little girls or round-eyed little boys crowded around the old man on the porch, where he'd gotten in the habit of sitting every afternoon.

Grandpa smiled in his gentle way and patiently answered their questions, or he'd tell them stories of brave warriors, ghosts, and animals, and the kids listened in awed silence. Those little guys thought Grandpa was great.

Finally, one day after school, my friends came home with me because nothing I said stopped them. "We're going to see the great Indian of Bell View Drive," said Hank, who was supposed to be my best friend. "My brother has seen him three times so he oughta be well enough to see us."

When we got to my house, Grandpa was sitting on the porch. He had on his red shirt, but today he also wore a fringed leather vest trimmed with beads. Instead of his usual cowboy boots, he had solidly beaded moccasins on his feet. Of course, he had his old black hat on—he was seldom without it. But it had been brushed, and the feather in the beaded headband was proudly erect, its tip a bright white. His hair lay in silver strands over the red shirt collar.

I stared just as my friends did, and I heard one of them murmur, "Wow!"

Grandpa looked up, and when his eyes met mine they twinkled as if he were laughing inside. He nodded to me, and my face got all hot. I could tell that he had known all along I was afraid he'd embarrass me in front of my friends.

"*Hau, hokšilas,* boys," he greeted and held out his hand.

My buddies passed in a single file and shook his hand as I introduced them. They were so polite I almost laughed. "How, Grandpa," and even a "How . . . do . . . you . . . do, sir."

"You look fine, Grandpa," I said as the guys sat down.

"*Hanh,* yes," he agreed. "When I woke up this morning, it seemed the right time to dress in the good clothes. I knew that my grandson would be bringing his friends."

"You guys want a soda or . . . ?" I offered, but no one answered. They were listening to Grandpa as he told how he'd killed the deer from which his vest was made.

Grandpa did most of the talking. I was proud of him and amazed at how respectfully quiet my friends were. Mom had to chase them home at supper time. As they left, they shook Grandpa's hand again and said to me, "Can we come back?"

But after they left, Mom said, "no more visitors for a while, Martin. Grandpa won't admit it, but his strength hasn't returned. He likes having company, but it tires him."

That evening Grandpa called me to his room before he went to sleep. "Tomorrow," he said, "when you come home, it will be time to give you the medicine bag."

I felt a hard squeeze from where my heart is supposed to be and was scared, but I answered, "OK, Grandpa."

All night I had weird dreams about thunder and lightning on a high hill. From a distance I heard the slow beat of a drum. When I woke up in the morning, I felt as if I hadn't slept at all. At school it seemed as if the day would never end, and when it finally did, I ran home.

Grandpa was in his room, sitting on the bed. The shades were down, and the place was dim and cool. I sat on the floor in front of Grandpa, but he didn't even look at me. After what seemed a long time, he spoke.

"I sent your mother and sister away. What you will hear today is only for your ears. What you will receive is only for your hands." He fell silent. I felt shivers down my back.

"My father in his early manhood," Grandpa began, "made a vision quest to find a spirit guide for his life. You cannot understand how it was in that time, when the great Teton Lakota were first made to stay on the reservation. There was a strong need for guidance from Wakantanka, the Great Spirit. But too many of the young men were filled with despair and hatred. They thought it was hopeless to search for a vision when the glorious life was gone and only the hated confines of a reservation lay ahead. But my father held to the old ways.

"He carefully prepared for his quest with a purifying sweat bath, and then he went alone to a high butte top to fast and pray. After three days he received his sacred dream—in which he found, after long searching, the white man's iron. He did not understand his vision of finding something belonging to the white people, for in that time they were the enemy. When he came down from the butte to cleanse himself at the stream below, he found the remains of a campfire and broken shell of an iron kettle. This was a sign that reinforced his dream. He took a piece of the iron for his medicine bag, which he had made of elk skin years before, to prepare for his quest.

"He returned to his village, where he told his dream to the wise old men of the tribe. They gave him the name Iron Shell, but they did not understand the meaning of the dream either. At first Iron Shell kept the piece of iron with him at all times and believed it gave him protection from the evils of those unhappy days.

"Then a terrible thing happened to Iron Shell. He and several other young men were taken from their homes by the soldiers and sent to a boarding school far from home. He was angry and lonesome for his parents and for the young girl he had wed before he was taken away. At first Iron Shell resisted the teachers' attempts to change him, and he did not try to learn. One day it was his turn to work in the school's blacksmith shop. As he walked into the place, he knew that his medicine had brought him there to learn and work with the white man's iron.

"Iron Shell became a blacksmith and worked at the trade when he returned to the reservation. All his life he treasured the medicine bag. When he was old and I was a man, he gave it to me."

Grandpa quit talking, and I stared in disbelief as he covered his face with his hands. His shoulders shook with quiet sobs. I looked away until he began to speak again.

"I kept the bag until my son, your mother's father, was a man and had to leave us to fight in the war across the ocean. I gave him the bag, for I believed it would protect him in battle, but he did not take it with him. He was afraid he would lose it. He died in a faraway land."

Again Grandpa was still, and I felt his grief around me.

"My son," he went on after clearing his throat, "had no sons, only one daughter, your mother. So the medicine bag must be passed to you."

He unbuttoned his shirt, pulled out the leather pouch, and lifted it over his head. He held it in his hand, turning it over and over as if memorizing how it looked.

"In the bag," he said, as he opened it and removed two objects, "is the broken shell of the iron kettle, a pebble from the butte, and a piece of the sacred sage." He held the pouch upside down and fine dust drifted out.

"After the bag is yours you must put a piece of prairie sage within and never open it again until you pass it on to your son." He replaced the pebble and the piece of iron and tied the bag.

I stood up, somehow knowing I should. Grandpa slowly rose from the bed and stood upright in front of me holding the bag before my face. I closed my eyes and waited for him to slip it over my head. But he spoke.

"No, you need not wear it." He placed the soft leather bag in my right hand and closed my other hand over it. "It would not be right to wear it in this time and place where no one will understand. Put it safely away until you are again on the reservation. Wear it then, when you replace the sacred sage."

Grandpa turned and sat again on the bed. Wearily he leaned his head against the pillow. "Go," he said. "I will sleep now."

"Thank you, Grandpa," I said softly and left with the bag in my hands.

That night Mom and Dad took Grandpa to the hospital. Two weeks later I stood alone on the lonely prairie of the reservation and put the sacred sage in my medicine bag.

The Twelve Moons

"Do you know what month it is?" Carmen asked as she ran into the house after school.

"September." Her mother looked up from the beads she was weaving on a small loom.

Yes, it is," Carmen answered. "But it's also the Moon When Leaves Are Turning Brown."

"Oh, you mean the Lakota name for the month," Carmen's mother said as she looked back at the loom. "Did your teacher tell you that?"

"Yes. Mrs. Black Lance asked us how we would name the month of September if we were going to give it a new name. She said in the old days the Indians didn't have a calendar like we have now. They named the time of the year after things that happened in nature or things that the people did. They had twelve different names, one for each time of the new moon."

"I'm glad you learned the Lakota name," Carmen's mother

said. "I knew them all once, but I think I've forgotten most of them now."

"Did you learn them in school?" asked Carmen.

"No, my grandmother taught them to me," said her mother. "But that was a long time ago, when I was younger than you are now."

"Why did you forget them?" asked Carmen.

"Well, I suppose I got so used to using the calendar names that I never thought about the Lakota ones," said her mother.

"I'll help you remember, Mom," Carmen said. "We're going to learn all of them in school. Before Mrs. Black Lance tells us the Lakota names, we have to make up our own names and see if they match the Indian ones."

After supper Carmen sat at the kitchen table and worked at the names until it was bedtime. "I have names for all the months except December, January, and February," she told her mother. "All I can think of is that those months are cold and we have snow all the time."

"Well," her mother said, "think about what happens besides snow. What does your dad do in December?"

Carmen thought a minute and clapped her hands as she remembered. "He goes deer hunting." She quickly wrote on her paper.

"Now, January," she said as she chewed on her pencil eraser. "All I can think of is that you drive me to the bus stop, so I can wait in the warm car and not out in the cold wind."

"January is usually our coldest month," agreed her mother.

Carmen wrote and then said, "But February is cold, too. And then it seems like winter will never end."

"I think that tells about February very well," smiled her mother.

Carmen smiled, too, as she finished her list. "There," she said, holding up the list, "tomorrow I'll find out how close my names are to the Lakota ones."

The next day after school, Carmen's mother wanted to know about the names.

"See," Carmen said, holding out a paper, "on the left I copied the Lakota names and the reasons for each one. The names I thought of are on the right."

LAKOTA NAMES

MY NAMES

LAKOTA NAMES	MY NAMES
January—Moon of the Terrible	Moon When It Is the Coldest
February—Moon When There Is Frost Inside the Lodge (*The people had to stay in the tipis all the time, and their breathing made the walls all frosty.*)	Moon When Winter Is Too Long
March—Moon When the Frost Covers the Prairie Chickens' Eyes (*The weather gets warmer but then it turns cold, and the poor prairie chickens wake up with frost on their eyelids.*)	Moon When Spring Begins, But It Snows Again
April—Moon When the Geese Return (*The people were glad to see the geese come back because they were hungry after the long winter.*)	Moon When the Robins Come Back
May—Moon When the Leaves Are Green	Moon When the Trees Get Leaves

June—two names:

Moon When Strawberries Are Ripe (*in the woods*)	Moon When the Wild Roses Bloom
Moon When Wild Turnips Bloom (*in the prairie*)	

July—Moon When the Chokecherries Are Ripe   Moon When We Pick Chokecherries

August—Moon When All Things Ripen   Moon When Mom Dries Corn

September—Moon When the Leaves Are Turning Brown   (*I already knew it*)

October—Moon When Dead Leaves Are Snapping and Are Shaken Off in the Wind   Moon When the Leaves Fall Off the Trees

November—Moon When Winter Sets In   Moon When It First Snows

December—Moon When Horns Are Broken Off (*deer horns*)   Moon When Dad Brings Home a Deer

"Your names are good ones," Carmen's mother agreed.

"Yes," Carmen said proudly.

"Mine aren't exactly like the Lakota ones, but close. I guess that's 'cause the weather and what we do at certain times of the year are not much different from the days when the Lakota lived in tipis."

Clean Hands

Marie and Joe didn't know what to do. They were tired of playing the same old games they'd invented during the summer. Their favorite pastime was to take turns playing house with Marie's doll, then they'd be cowboys with Joe's gun. Today Joe's gun was broken, and Marie said her doll was sick.

"Go outdoors," Mama had said. "Play in the sun. School will be starting soon and then you'll wish you could be outside."

The children always played outdoors anyway, so they knew Mama wanted them out of the way while she cleaned the house. Now they were sitting under the old oak tree in the yard.

"Tell me about school, Joe," Marie said.

Joe was going to be in the second grade, and Marie, who would be going to school for the first time, was anxious to know what school was like.

"Aw," said Joe. "There's not much to tell. You have to get up early and wash, even if you bathed the night before. You eat, then walk to the road to wait for the bus. The bus ride is fun. When you get to school you line up to go to the bathroom, and then you wash again. It seems like you have to be so clean to go to school. Wash, wash, wash all the time!" Joe was disgusted.

Joe really liked school, but he hated to take the time to always wash his hands.

"Why do you have to be so clean, Joe?" asked Marie.

A soft laugh interrupted their talk. They peeked around the other side of the tree and saw Grandma sitting there sorting chokecherries from a large tin bucket.

"Come," Grandma said, "sit by me. We will talk about being clean while you help me sort the stems and leaves from the cherries."

Joe and Marie moved to her side. They were glad Grandma was there. She sometimes told them stories when there wasn't anything else to do.

"OK, Grandma," Joe said as he sat down, "why do we have to be so clean to go to school?" He really didn't want to be convinced that it was a good thing.

"Do you ever wash when you don't have school?" asked Grandma.

"Well, yes," Joe said reluctantly. "You and Mama make us wash our hands before we eat, and we have to bathe. But when school is on it seems like we have to wash more."

Grandma chuckled softly again and asked, "Do you know why we sort the cherries?"

"To take out the leaves, stems, and bugs before you dry the cherries," answered Marie.

"We can't eat leaves," Joe said.

"Yeah, who wants to eat a dirty old leaf—or a bug," Marie agreed, making a face.

Clean Hands   19

The old lady smiled, "What will we do with the cherries after they are sorted?"

"Wash them," Joe answered. Then he put his hand over his mouth and laughed after saying the hated word.

"Yes," Grandma said, "we pick out all of the stems, leaves, and bugs that we can see, then we rinse the cherries in clean water to wash out the things we can't see. If the leaves and stems are dirty, the cherries must be too."

"Yeah," said Marie, "who wants to eat dirt!"

"See our old dog by the porch? He is sitting so sadly by himself watching us." Grandma said. "Why don't you call the dog and play with him?"

"No," the children exclaimed, "he stinks!"

Grandma laughed, "When do you like to play with him?"

"After he goes swimming in the creek and he's clean."

"Um," Grandma murmured. "Do you remember when Cat had kittens."

"Oh, yes," said Marie. "They were so soft and cute."

"Remember how Cat took care of them?" asked Grandma.

"Yes," answered Joe. "She was always licking the kittens. I thought she'd wear out her tongue."

"Why did she lick them?"

"I know," laughed Marie. "She was washing them, wasn't she, Grandma?"

"Oh, boy!" said Joe in disgust.

"Even animals know it is good to be clean," Grandma said, glancing at Joe.

Joe was quiet. He knew that Grandma had been directing their talk to the subject of being clean even if she hadn't come right out and said so.

"What's animals washing got to do with my having to bathe

all the time?" Joe challenged. "I'm not a cat or a dog. Besides," he added, "Old Man Thunder never takes a bath. I know!"

"How do you know?" asked Grandma with a twinkle in her eyes.

Joe had to look away when he answered quietly, "Because he doesn't smell so good."

"We Lakota have not always had the kind of soap we have today, or well-water; but we have had our own ways of keeping ourselves clean. There have always been streams to bathe in during the summer and snow to melt in the winter."

"Old Man Thunder never bathes," Joe stubbornly insisted.

"Yeah," said Marie, "and that's why he doesn't smell so good. Besides he has sores and his eyes are all runny."

"He is an old, old man," said Grandma. "He can't see very well and isn't able to get around like he used to when he was young. "We'll tell the Tribal Health Committee about him, and they'll send someone to see him. It's because of things called germs that the old man has sores and his eyes are infected.

"Germs are so small that we can't see them; but when we wash ourselves, we also wash away the germs that can 'cause sores or that could make us sick."

The children were quiet, thinking about what Grandma had said. Joe admitted to himself that there might be a good reason for washing, but he sure wasn't going to say so out loud.

Marie suddenly held up her hands that were stained from the cherries. "Look at your hands, Joe," she said.

"Oh, boy," said Joe holding out his hands. "They have cherry spots all over. Now I'll have to wash them!"

Marie and Grandma laughed as he stomped away to the house.

The Slim Butte Ghost

"We've seen the ghost again," Mr. High Bear calmly announced. "Up on the Slim," he nodded his head north toward the butte jutting out of the prairie.

Hank looked up, wondering if Mr. High Bear was serious. "A real ghost?" he wanted to ask, but one thing he had learned from Grandpa this summer was that it wasn't necessary to rush conversation or anything else in Indian country. So Hank kept his mouth shut and tried to sit still and quiet while the neighbor and Grandpa visited.

"How long's it been?" Grandpa asked.

"Must be ten, twelve years," Mr. High Bear sipped coffee, eyes squinted in thought. "Can't be the same one."

"No," agreed Grandpa.

Hank blew into his mug of steaming coffee to keep from blurting out the questions racing in his head. He sipped and gasped back a yelp as the scalding brew burned his tongue.

"Going after him?" Grandpa asked, still gazing out of the window.

Mr. High Bear nodded.

"Guess I won't be going this time," Grandpa smiled, but Hank, blowing air over his smarting tongue, heard the yearning in the old man's voice.

"Where'd you hunt before?" Mr. High Bear asked, eyes on the butte.

"All over the damn hill," Grandpa chuckled.

Mr. High Bear smiled and Hank almost spilled the coffee as the man asked, "Your *takoža* want to come?"

Instantly, as the men turned to him, Hank closed his mouth over his painful tongue. "He ain't been on a horse this visit," Grandpa said, giving Hank a quizzical glance.

"I can ride," Hank blurted out.

"Joe's going, too," Mr. High Bear said, referring to his son, who was about Hank's age. "He hasn't been on a long ride like this'll be, so you'll both be in the same shape."

Mr. High Bear nodded, "They'll get along." He stood. "We'll start about eight in the morning. We'll bring a horse for you. Better pack a bedroll."

Hank nodded, trying not to show his excitement, but after Mr. High Bear had left, the questions he'd held back tumbled out.

"What white stallion? Where are we going?"

"You'll be hunting the Slim Butte ghost." Grandpa pointed ahead of them toward a narrow, flat-topped hill that rose steeply out of the prairie. Hank could see why it was called "Slim."

"What do you mean, *ghost?*"

Grandpa stared at the butte. "I was a young man when I first saw it," he mused. "Older folks used to tell about a ghost that appeared every so often on or around Slim Butte. They said it was big and white and that it would jump up in front of a horse and rider from out of nowhere, scare 'em silly, and then take off like lightning.

"One morning before sunrise, Nelly was taking me over to a branding job. Just as it started to get light, we rode into fog in the lowlands along the creek below the butte. It was so thick, I could barely see Nelly's ears, so we slowed to a walk.

"I started whistling to keep myself company, then stopped 'cause I remembered what the elders used to say about whistling calling up ghosts."

Hank waited for Grandpa to go on, but the old man was nodding his head and chuckling at his memories. Finally he said, "I was scared, but then the sun lightened up the mist, and I kicked Nelly into a trot. I didn't want to be late for my job. Just as we topped a rise, I saw it. A pale thing, whiter than the fog that drifted in wisps in the breeze that come up. Nelly saw it too. She reared up, almost throwing me. She danced around, and I hung on, but all the while I kept watching what I really thought was a ghost.

"It lit out—so fast it was a blur, and Nelly took after it. I was too busy hanging on while trying to rein her in. Nelly was sure-footed, but she was running low to the ground at her racing pace. The fog was lifting, but it was still hard to see. I feared she'd step in a gopher or prairie-dog hole and break a leg—besides what I might break if she went down.

"But I couldn't stop her. I wondered if that ghost hadn't put spell on Nelly to run her to death. Then the fog cleared.

"In the bright morning sun, I saw it wasn't a ghost Nelly was chasing; it was the biggest white stallion I'd ever seen. I didn't blame Nelly for going after him."

Grandpa fell silent, and Hank urged, "So, what happened?"

"Well, I wanted to go after the stallion—see if I could capture him. What a grand catch he'd be. He'd be an easy rider with those long legs, and he'd sire a herd of beautiful horses. But Nelly was played out; she was a quarter horse, only good for top speed for a quarter of a mile. She'd never catch up with that stallion that looked like he could run forever."

"Did you ever try to find him again?"

"Sure did. When I got to my job I told the boss and the other hands, and they had a laugh over a horse being mistaken for a ghost. But the boss, one of the first white ranchers in the area, had seen the stallion when he'd first settled there. He was alone then, but he always hoped to sight the stallion again and, with help, go after him.

"We didn't do any branding the next two days. We went hunting for the stallion instead, but he was gone, vanished.

About every ten years or so, somebody sights him again. 'Course it can't be the same one—probably descendents of the one I saw, because white colts have been seen in the wild herd.

Once, so the story goes, such a colt was caught along with some others, but during the night there was a big ruckus at the corral holding 'em. By the time the men got out to see what caused it, the wild horses had run off. Some think the big stallion came to free his colt. But each time the stallion is sighted, a bunch rides out and hopes to catch him."

Grandpa sighed and gazed at the butte looming in the distance. "I've been on every hunt 'cept now. Don't think my rusty old bones can handle this one." He gave a rueful laugh, and Hank knew he wanted to go.

"Come on," Grandpa said, rising stiffly from his chair. "Let's see what we can fix up for a bedroll."

He pulled an old trunk away from the wall, opened it, and pulled out a blue, wool blanket that had two stripes on one end. "Whew, stinks of mothballs. Better hang it out on the line to air before we roll it up. This was my grandpa's blanket," he explained. "It replaced his buffalo robe."

"Do you think I should take it?" Hank was concerned. "What if I . . . what if something happens to it?"

"It's tough," Grandpa said, "and it'll keep you warmer than any new sleeping bag, but it won't be easy sleeping on the ground."

"I'll be OK, Grandpa. If you could sleep on the ground, I can," Hank reassured Grandpa and himself, too.

"Sure you can. But the ride's going to be rough—longer and harder than any riding you've ever done. Think you can handle it?"

"Sure," Hank said calmly, despite the anxious excitement that dried his mouth.

The evening had turned chill, and even though bedtime was early and he was excited about the day to come, Hank had no trouble sleeping.

He awakened to Grandpa's stirring in the kitchen and checked his watch to see that it was seven o'clock. He was glad Grandpa didn't have to call him to get up. He quickly dressed and ate the eggs, bacon, and toast Grandpa had ready. Just as he finished, Mr. High Bear, Joe, and two other men rode up with sleeping bags tightly rolled and tied to their saddles along with other nylon bags bulging with provisions and gear for a night's camp.

Joe led Babe, a saddled and bridled old mare, who munched grass while Hank tied his blanket roll and a plastic bottle of water to the saddle. Hank was disappointed in the mare but knew that she'd been picked because she was an easy rider that would suit his inexperience.

He mounted and followed the others, leaving Grandpa wistfully watching. Hank felt sorry that Grandpa couldn't come but knew the old man accepted that chasing stallions was for the young and strong.

The men and Joe rode abreast, and Hank tried to kick Babe into line with them. But she kept her own pace in the rear.

After about an hour's ride they reached the creek below the butte and Hank was glad to dismount. Despite Babe's gentle gait, his tailbone was sore and the muscles in his inner thighs ached from being stretched over the saddle.

He did what the others did: watered the horses before they drank themselves. Horses grazed as the men rested and munched trail food they shared with Hank.

After about twenty minutes, Mr. High Bear stood. "We'll scout the base of the butte to see if there's any sign of the ghost. Don't think we'll spot him today; most sightings have been at dawn. As we go, check for cattle and we'll herd them out of there so we won't have to worry about them getting in the way tomorrow in case we do find the stallion."

They found four cows with calves that they herded back toward the High Bear ranch but found no sign of the ghost horse. They made camp where they'd rested in the morning. This time Hank had to stifle a groan as he dismounted, wanting only to collapse on the ground, but he unsaddled and watered the horses before he could rest.

He had a unreal sense of watching himself in a Western, but Joe had to show him how to halter and hobble Babe so that she would be easy to catch in the morning. Hank thought, "If this were a movie, I'd be the greenhorn—like I really am!"

Still, the feeling of being a different person in another time stuck with Hank as he and Joe gathered dry wood for the cook fire.

Hank didn't try to talk to Joe. He was too tired, but Joe spoke. "Ever camped out before?"

"Sure," Hank replied.

"Where?"

"At home, along the river," Hank didn't add that it had been YMCA camp.

They carried the wood to Mr. High Bear, who had dug a fire pit and ringed it with rocks. Hank half expected Mr. High Bear to use flint or twirl fire sticks to start the fire, but he didn't even use matches. He flicked a butane lighter and the dry twigs and wood flared.

The sense of time past was dispelled when they ate their supper of rehydrated stew off paper plates and when they drank from foam cups. The trash was thrown in the fire, and there were no dishes to wash, like Grandpa told of doing in his youth. Grandpa also drank right from the creek, but that wasn't safe to do anymore.

Hank spread his blankets on the ground as the others unrolled their sleeping bags. "People sure have gotten soft," he thought as he watched Mr. High Bear put a foam pad under his bag. Well, Hank was going to sleep the way Grandpa used to do, with the ground for a mattress, but he didn't use his saddle for a pillow since no one else did. He lay with his arms under his head and watched the stars come out.

Nearby, Joe zipped his sleeping bag. "What grade you in?" he asked Hank.

"Going to be a junior."

"Me too."

Hank, arms numbing under his head, rolled to his side.

"You sore from riding?"

"Some," Hank admitted.

"Gonna be worse tomorrow," Joe stated flatly.

"Probably," Hank agreed and shifted his hips off a rock.

"Should be fun," Joe said and settled into his sleeping bag, rustling the nylon. "This is my first hunt. I was too little last time."

Those were the most words Hank had ever heard Joe speak at one time, so he thought he'd better keep up the conversation since Joe wanted to talk. "Do you think we'll catch him?"

"No," Joe answered after a moment, his voice muffled by his sleeping bag.

Hank shifted, tucking his feet under the blanket. It was getting cold, and he was painfully aware of his aching muscles on the hard ground. He heard the horses chomping grass and one of the men cough. A slight breeze blew smoke from the dying fire, making his eyes smart. He curled into a ball, tucking the blanket over his head.

He slept soundly but was jolted awake by the blast of a loud, piercing trumpet. Confused, he tried to jump up, but his feet tangled in the blanket. Mr. High Bear and the other men shouted and swore as they struggled out of their sleeping bags.

Hank recognized Babe's whinny among the other horses' as they restlessly stomped in their hobbles. Then the hair on the nape of his neck bristled as the wild, trumpetlike call sounded again and pounding hooves seemed to head right for him.

He stumbled stiffly to where the men were struggling to hold the hobbled horses. Even old Babe was rearing and tossing her head. Hank grabbed her halter and was almost jerked from his feet as she pulled away.

Galloping hooves faded into the night, but the call came again, fainter and farther off. "OK, girl, OK," Hank calmed Babe and stoked her neck until the tremors rippling her hide stilled.

"She'll stay now," Mr. High Bear's voice made Hank jump. "The stallion's gone."

"The stallion? Was that the sound?" He wasn't sure what to call the eerie, wild trumpeting that had roused him.

"Yes, he was calling the mares," Mr. High Bear said. "He sure is a nervy one," he chuckled. "Almost into camp before we woke up."

"Did you see him?"

"No, just heard him."

Hank smoothed the blanket wrapped snugly about him, then saw that Joe was still snoring in his warm sleeping bag. He'd slept though the noise and confusion.

Hank had no trouble getting back to sleep. The stallion's visit during the night could have been part of a dream of a ghost horse suddenly appearing in the morning fog. When he awoke again it was to a morning mist swirling damp and cold around the camp.

Hank rolled his blanket and enviously watched Joe crawl warm and dry from his sleeping bag. Joe grinned sheepishly when the men teased him about sleeping through the stallion's visit.

After a breakfast of dry granola bars washed down with water, the horses were saddled and bridled, the gear was packed, and Hank climbed stiffly into the saddle.

Babe stayed in her end place as they rode single file through the fog and up the butte. The trail traversed the slope and Hank again felt the displaced sensation of seeing himself in a dream world. At times his head broke through the fog into blinding sunlight and he could see the tops of Babe's twitching ears, but all else was wrapped in a damp, misty blanket. He rode above the fog onto the sunlit summit, an enchanted island in a sea of fluffy clouds.

Enthralled, he watched the fog disperse in ragged, shifting streamers uncovering the rough slope of the butte below him.

"Hey!" Hank heard Joe call and saw him wave to keep up. He kicked Babe to follow Joe down the far trail.

Slowly, Babe lurched stiff-legged down the slope, every jolting step jarring Hank's spine. Then she snorted, jerked her head, and shoved up against the rump of Joe's horse as the stallion's piercing trumpet called.

Hank clutched the saddle horn with one hand, tightly grasping Babe's reins as she swerved and shoved to pass Joe's pinto. "Ow!" Hank exclaimed as the pinto's lashing hooves painfully jabbed his leg.

The wild command sounded again, and now all of the horses were in turmoil, while the men yelled and tried to keep the beasts on the trail. Hank struggled with Babe, fighting for control as she lurched past the pinto and broke, racing past the others on the flat.

Hank's right foot slipped out of the bouncing stirrup. Frantic, he pulled back on the reins. "Thought she'd step in a gopher or prairie-dog hole," Grandpa's voice burned in his mind.

"Hold her!" Mr. High Bear yelled, racing after the runaway.

Hank's scrabbling foot finally found the stirrup, and he forced himself to sit back in the saddle, brace his feet, and pull harder.

Babe tossed her head, fighting the bit, but her run gradually slowed to a jouncing trot that threatened to unseat Hank. "Whoa! Whoa!" he called, steadily tightening the reins. Babe walked and finally stopped.

Hank, as sweaty as the horse, panted breathlessly, his racing heart beating loudly in his ears. He was light-headed, near to hyperventilating. He managed to take a deep breath then slowly exhale, repeating this until the roaring in his ears stopped and he knew he wouldn't faint.

"Old Babe thought she was a filly again," Mr. High Bear laughed as he caught up with Hank. "Ain't seen her run like that for years." His voice was light, but his look was serious as he gazed at Hank's pale face.

Hank managed a weak smile, not trusting his voice to speak. Mr. High Bear nodded, and he was grateful that the man hadn't said anything about Babe being a runaway, which would have implied that the raw boy couldn't control the old mare.

They rode on, circling the butte, but didn't hear or see the stallion again. About noon, they gave up and headed back to Grandpa's.

"Didn't get him?" Grandpa smiled at Mr. High Bear who shook his head.

"Didn't think you would," Grandpa said and everyone but Hank laughed.

"What's so funny?" Then he understood. No one—Grandpa, Mr. High Bear, Joe—none of them had expected to catch the stallion. It was a ritual that had to be repeated each time the stallion appeared. Hank's spine tingled, every muscle in his body ached, and his leg throbbed, but he felt good about being a part of the hunt.

Stiffly he swung off Babe, hanging onto the saddle to stay upright as pain shot through his leg.

"Your takoža did OK," Mr. High Bear told Grandpa.

"Knew he would, "Grandpa nodded, "and now he knows you can't catch a ghost."

Jimmy Yellow Hawk

"Grandpa, I don't want to be called Little Jim anymore. How can I change my name?"

Grandpa cleared his throat and asked, "Why don't you want to be called Little Jim?"

The boy was a bit embarrassed as he answered, "The other kids tease me about being a little kid because of the 'Little' in my name."

"Your name is the same as your father's—James. Since he is older and had the name first, he is Big Jim and you are Little."

"I know," said the boy, kicking a rock on the ground. "But I still want to change my name."

"Your parents could have called you Junior—would that be better?"

Little Jim shook his head. "That still means a smaller Jim."

"Hmm," Grandpa thought. "So, you want a more grown-up name?"

Little Jim nodded. Grandpa cleared his throat and said, "In the old days, there was an Indian boy your age who got a new name because of a brave thing he did.

"It was in the time of the long cold winter when there was more snow than any of the old people had ever known. The men hunted but found no game. The only food the people had was the corn the women had dried in the summer. Soon that was almost gone. The people were starving, so one of the younger and stronger men made the long trip to see the government man at the agency. He hoped the man would give him some food for the people. He returned with a bag of corn and nothing more.

"Soon after the young man returned he got sick. It was a coughing sickness he had caught from the agency people. It wasn't long before others were sick and the men became too weak to hunt.

"There was a boy in the tribe who didn't get sick. His grandfather had taught him how to make snares to trap small animals. The boy had not been allowed to do any real trapping because the winter was so bad and his mother was afraid that he would get lost in a blizzard.

"When no one could go hunting, the boy decided that he would go down along the creek and set some snares. Maybe he could trap an animal they could eat. The boy did not tell anyone of his plan. He left the tipi in the morning while it was still dark and no one was awake.

"He went to the creek and then almost went home because it was so strange and different with the snow covering everything. He was scared, but he looked carefully along the bank and found tracks, so he knew that animals had been there. He set his snares and went home before anyone found out that he had been gone.

"The next morning he again left before anyone was awake. He checked his snares and found that he had caught two rabbits. He was happy and ran back to his tipi with the rabbits. His family was very proud of him and his mother made a stew with the rabbits and the corn from the agency. The stew gave needed strength to the hunters who were then able to go hunting again."

Grandpa paused to sip his coffee. He continued. "The whole band was very proud of the brave boy. In the spring when all were well and healthy again, a council was called and a feast was held to honor the boy.

"A deer was cooked for all the people and there was singing and dancing long into the night. At the end of the celebration the boy was given a new name. He was known as Goes Alone in the Morning and was not considered a little boy anymore but as one who was growing to be a man."

Little Jim liked the story and wished he had lived in the old times so that he could do a brave thing and not be called Little Jim anymore. Grandpa yawned and stretched so that Little Jim knew it was time to go to bed.

Little Jim dreamed about Goes Alone in the Morning, but in his dream he was the brave boy.

The summer was almost over, school would soon be starting, and still Little Jim hadn't thought of anything to do to change his name. One day he and his father were cleaning out the barn, and hanging way up in a corner, Little Jim spied what looked like odd-shaped metal tools.

"Hey, Dad," he called, "what are those?"

Big Jim smiled, "Why, I'd forgotten about them. They're my traps. I used to go trapping when I was a boy about your age. They sure are rusty."

Little Jim got all excited, "Do they still work, Dad?"

"Why, sure they will," answered Big Jim. "All they need is to be cleaned and oiled."

"Do you suppose I could use them," Little Jim asked eagerly.

"I don't know why you couldn't," answered his father. "In fact, I think trapping would be a good thing for you to learn."

Little Jim carefully took down the traps, found a rag, and started rubbing at the rust. "Whoa," said Big Jim. "You can't do any trapping till winter. Let's finish the barn first, then we'll work on the traps. There's a lot you'll have to learn about using them before you can trap this winter."

On the first day of school Little Jim rode his horse to his friend Shasha's house. His friend was often teased about his reddish hair and called "red red," which is what his nickname meant.

But Shasha didn't seem to mind being teased, like Little Jim did.

Little Jim told Shasha of his plan to do some trapping in the winter. Maybe I'll catch a wolf or a bobcat and get an Indian name for doing a brave thing."

Shasha laughed, "Bobcats and wolves never get caught in traps, you dummy!"

Little Jim was hurt.

"Oh, all you'll probably get are rabbits," teased Shasha.

Little Jim felt bad that his friend didn't think much of his plan, but he was still going to do it. "Well, they might!" he said.

He'd show Shasha!

That evening after school Little Jim told Grandpa of his plan to be a trapper. Grandpa was pleased that Little Jim was going to learn how to trap but said it wouldn't be the same as Goes Alone in the Morning because Little Jim's family wasn't starving.

Now Little Jim was confused about the whole thing. He asked if it would be a brave thing if he trapped a bobcat or wolf.

"You will be using traps for small animals," answered Grandpa. "Bobcats or wolves are usually too smart to get caught in such traps."

"But could they?" insisted Little Jim.

"It's possible," answered Grandpa, "but if it did happen you would have to be very careful because they become vicious and very dangerous when trapped."

Grandpa went on to explain that there was bounty money for wolves and bobcats because they preyed on calves and sheep.

"What kind of a name would I get if I did catch one of them?" Little Jim asked.

"That," answered Grandpa, "would depend on how hard a job it was and how much the bounty was."

Grandpa smiled and went on, "You can trap rabbits. Some people buy their pelts, and they also make good stew."

Little Jim didn't think much of that idea. "I might be called Rabbit Boy if that's all I caught."

Big Jim went with him along the creek bottom and showed Little Jim the best places to set the traps.

"You have to pick a sheltered spot," he explained, "out of the wind where the snow won't drift in."

Little Jim listened carefully because he wanted to learn all he could so that he could trap by himself.

If Little Jim ever did trap a bobcat he was to leave it alone and get his father to help.

As soon as the first snows fell that winter, Little Jim took down his traps. After school, he rode his pony along the same places he'd checked for stray cattle in the summer, but now the snow made it all look different. He set his traps in the sheltered places along the creek that he and Big Jim had chosen.

All the next day in school he had trouble sitting still and paying attention to his lessons. He was so eager to get home he didn't even wait for Shasha, who yelled after him as he galloped out of the schoolyard.

"Hey, what's your hurry?"

"Gotta check my traps," Little Jim yelled back.

"Get your rabbits you mean," laughed Shasha.

But Little Jim didn't care and he hurried home. "Mama," he called as he rushed into the house, "I'm going to check my traps."

"Can't you say hello," Mama chided. "Don't you want a cookie or something to eat before you go? It will be a while before supper."

"Oh, yeah, hi!" said Little Jim. He stuffed cookies into the pocket of his parka and grabbed a burlap bag in which he would carry the animals home.

"Gotta hurry," he said, "see you later!"

That first day was disappointing, for he didn't trap a thing. But he carefully checked all of the traps and went home positive that the next day he would get something. Little Jim worked hard at trapping all winter. It never took him very long to check his lines because he rode his pony. Over his saddle was the bag to put the animals in. But, as Shasha had predicted, he caught only rabbits, and he was becoming discouraged. Grandpa liked rabbit stew and thought it was a good thing for Little Jim to trap rabbits. Although no one called him Rabbit Boy, he was still Little Jim, and it seemed to him that a trapper should have a better name.

One evening after school, when he'd been trapping for about

two months, it was so bitterly cold and windy that Little Jim's mother didn't want him to go out to check his traps.

But Little Jim was sure that he must have caught something because there were unusual tracks, different from a rabbit's, around his traps.

He bundled up in his new parka and set out. The wind was blowing hard on his back as he rode and he was glad that he didn't have to ride into it. The first trap was empty, so he guided the pony through the deep snow to the next one. He had almost reached the brush where he had set it when he smelled the strong stink of skunk.

He reined in short. The pony danced around nervously and tried to turn toward home. Little Jim dismounted and walked cautiously to the trap. He didn't want to get any closer because of the awful stink, but he forced himself to move.

The skunk was lying still in the trap, and Little Jim let out the breath he had been holding. He knelt down to release the animal, but as he reached for the trap the skunk suddenly moved and Little Jim almost fell into the icy creek. The pony gave a loud whinny of fright and took off for home. Little Jim ran after it.

Little Jim's eyes hurt, his nose and lungs burned, and the awful stink was everywhere.

Coughing and gagging, with tears streaming from his eyes, Little Jim ran. He felt like throwing up.

Big Jim had finished chores in the barn and was in the yard when the pony ran through the gate. It had never come home alone before, and Big Jim knew something was wrong. He rushed into the house, grabbed his rifle and yelled, "I'm going out to look for Little Jim!"

He caught the pony and was about to mount it when he saw

Little Jim floundering through the snow into the yard. Little Jim couldn't speak, but the skunk-stink reached Big Jim before the boy did.

"Stop right there!" Big Jim ordered.

The boy was trying not to cry, especially since Grandpa had come outside and Mama peered out the door. She was holding her nose.

"Get a bath ready, Marie. Little Jim needs one!"

Big Jim made his son walk in front of him back to the place of the trapped skunk. From a safe distance, he shot the skunk. Little Jim released the animal, even as he gagged and retched at the terrible odor.

Big Jim handed him a length of twine he'd found in this pocket. "Hang it in a tree. In a few days we'll come back to get it—after the worst of the smell is gone."

At home, Big Jim told his son to go to the old shed behind the house where Mama and Grandpa had a tub of steaming hot water and soap waiting. Little Jim undressed and threw his clothes out the door. It was icy cold in the shed. Little Jim shivered, then gasped and jerked his foot back from the steaming hot water. But he lowered himself into the tub and Jim scrubbed himself all over. His mother wrapped him in a towel and a blanket, and Big Jim carried him into the house where Grandpa had warm pajamas and a chair waiting by the stove.

Big Jim had to pile all of the boy's clothes in the backyard, pour kerosene over the pile, and burn it because the skunk smell would never come out.

Little Jim, clean and not so smelly anymore, was terribly unhappy. Neither Grandpa nor his father had scolded him, but he knew his mother was upset about the expensive new parka that had to be burned.

Mama made hot chocolate for him and coffee for everybody else. They all sat around the stove not saying anything and then Grandpa cleared his throat as he usually did before starting to tell a story.

The story, this time, was about an Indian boy who didn't like his name and who wanted to change it because he thought he wasn't a little boy anymore. The boy had worked hard all winter learning to be a trapper and brought home many rabbits that made good stew. The boy had learned many things about trapping and his family was proud of him.

The boy had learned in a very hard way that it wasn't necessary to trap a big dangerous animal, like a bobcat, to have trouble. This boy hadn't earned a great name as Goes Alone in the Morning had, but neither did Lakota boys of today earn Indian names for deeds of valor in the old way.

Little Jim knew Grandpa was telling the story about him, but he said nothing.

Grandpa continued his story, "Now in the old way, this boy would have been given a name as a result of what had happened with the not-so-dangerous animal. Such a name might be Skunk Face, and he would have to go by that name whether he liked it or not. In the old way, when the people heard the name Skunk Face they would know right away how he had gotten his name."

Little Jim hung his head, but Grandpa went on.

"In the old way the boy would have to work very hard to show that he had learned from his experience. He would know that it is best to ride with the wind in his face when nearing a trap. He would know that he should never get close to the trap until he was sure the animal was dead."

Grandpa turned to Little Jim. "I think the name Little Jim is no longer right for you because you have learned many things as a trapper and provided your family with much good food this winter. But would you want to be named Skunk Face in the old way?"

Little Jim snuffled and wiped his nose. He shook his head. "No, I'd rather stay Little Jim."

His father put a hand on his son's shoulder. "When I was a boy I was called Jimmy. That is not a grand as Goes Alone in the Morning," then he smiled, "or as fancy as Skunk Face, but it would show that you are growing up."

"But the other kids will still call me Little Jim," he protested, wiping tears away.

"That," said his father," is not important because you know and we know that you are not a little kid anymore."

Mama rose and took the empty cups. "That's enough excitement for today," she said. "It's time for our boy, no matter what his name is, to go to bed." She gave him a hug before he went to his room.

"I think Jimmy is a fine name for a big boy," said Mama.

During the rest of the winter, Big Jim went out more often to help his son. He taught Little Jim where to look for rabbits and how to identify their tracks and tell them apart from the spoor of skunks and other wild creatures that sometimes foraged near the creek.

Little Jim came to know the special hunting grounds of all the animals that visited the creek. One day he pleased his father by recognizing the telltale signs left behind by a muskrat that had been digging for roots near the bank. Big Jim said, "If there were still mink around, that muskrat would be lucky to last through the winter."

"But minks are too tiny to hunt muskrats, aren't they?" Little Jim wanted to know.

"Don't you believe it," his father said. "Minks are lethal. They'll strike at anything that moves. Remember, they belong to the weasel family—the deadliest animals for their size that we know."

Mama was waiting supper for them one evening when Little Jim came bursting into the house, so excited that he didn't make much sense.

Mama and Grandpa grabbed their coats and went outside to see what all the commotion was about.

Big Jim, smiling very proudly, was holding up a mink for them to see. "See what our trapper got?"

"Oh, my," said Mama.

Grandpa said, "*waśte!*" Both were very impressed. Mink had been scarce in the area for a long time and it was unusual for one to be trapped.

"Where did you get it, L'il . . . Jimmy?" asked Grandpa.

"In the same place I got the skunk," he answered, and they all laughed.

Big Jim helped skin and tan the pelt and then they took it to town. Big Jim was sure it would sell for enough money to buy a new parka.

The store was filled with people as they walked in. Shasha and his father were sitting on blocks of salt and greeted the Yellow Hawks warmly.

Big Jim placed the bag with the mink in it on the counter and took the pelt out when Mr. Haycock came over. "Hey, a mink!" the storekeeper said. He picked it up and carefully examined it. "They've been mighty scarce for a long time."

He held it up for all in the store to see, "Looks like a prime one, too. Where'd you trap it?" he asked.

Big Jim turned and spoke loud enough for everyone to hear, "My son, Jimmy, trapped it!" he said with pride in his voice.

"You don't say," said Mr. Haycock. He reached over to shake Jimmy's hand. "Boy, you're growing up! Congratulations."

To the others in the store he announced, "Hey, look here. Jimmy Yellow Hawk trapped this mink. Isn't that something?"

Jimmy couldn't stop grinning. He was happy about what he had done, but what pleased him more was that no one, not even Shasha, called him Little Jim. He had become Jimmy to everyone.

Grandpa Was a Cowboy and an Indian

I got acquainted with my grandpa last summer. Oh, I knew him before as my grandfather and as my mom's dad, but I finally got to know him as a person.

I'd visited Grandpa and Grandma in other summers with my folks when I was little kid. I liked going to their small ranch on the Rosebud Reservation in South Dakota, where my mom grew up. Grandpa was always busy working during those few weeks, but he took time to teach me how to ride a horse, and when I got bigger he even let me help him with the cattle and the haying. So by the time I was in high school, Grandpa had taught me how to do a lot of things most people in the city only read about.

Of course, I didn't think of helping Grandpa as work. It was fun, and I loved being out-of-doors. But running a ranch for a man of Grandpa's age was tiring work, and come evening he went to bed early while the rest of us sat and visited.

Grandpa finally retired from working the ranch. He and Grandma still lived out there along Little Oak Creek, but they rented the hay and grazing land to a neighbor. Even after Grandma died, Grandpa insisted on staying there by himself.

After I got into high school I usually had a summer job and didn't go to visit Grandpa when my folks did. But last summer I couldn't find a job, so Mom and Dad sent me to Grandpa's. "You'll be company for him," they said, "and you can get a job helping one of the ranchers out there."

I fussed about going. "There won't be anything to do at Grandpa's," I complained. But deep down I was glad they made me go. I liked the wide openness of the reservation prairies and being able to see for miles without having my view blocked by tall buildings. I wanted to see stars that filled up the sky un-dimmed by city lights. The air would be clear and clean. The only sound would be the wind in the oak trees. I wouldn't miss the city traffic smell and noise.

So I went, and it was a great summer. I got there in time for the first hay cutting and got a job with Grandpa's renter. After that was done I helped Grandpa paint the house and outbuildings, and the renter hired me for odd jobs when he needed help.

Grandpa and I didn't talk much during the day, but after supper Grandpa would build a fire in front of the house. There we'd sit and visit while we watched the steady flames brighten as the sky darkened.

Now, a year later, when I go to bed and close my eyes, I remember those evenings as clearly as if I were there again. And I hear Grandpa's deep raspy voice telling his stories. I don't remember them all, but the best come back as if Grandpa told them all in the same evening.

I rolled over on my back where I lay on the ground near

Grandpa. The stars were coming out, and the burning log settled in the fire and sent sparks up to them.

"How many times do you figure you've slept under the stars and by a fire like this?" I asked Grandpa, who sat in an old chair close enough to tend the fire.

"Thousands of times, I suppose," Grandpa answered quietly. "I can't begin to count the times I spent all night outdoors when I was a cowboy and," Grandpa chuckled, "when I was an Indian."

I laughed with him. "When you were an Indian did you wear feathers and have a tomahawk?" I asked, without really thinking he had.

"Once in a while I got dressed up like a warrior," Grandpa said. "But just on special occasions. I never had a tomahawk."

I sat up and looked at him, thinking he must be joking, but he looked serious so I asked, "When you were a cowboy did you wear boots and spurs?"

"Sure," Grandpa chuckled again. "But come evening I'd put on my soft old moccasins to rest my feet."

Grandpa gazed into the fire. I waited, but he seemed lost in faraway thoughts. Then he said, "When I was young, a person had to choose which he was going to be—white or Indian. Sometimes I used to get mixed up about it.

"I remember," he went on, "once when I was working with both Indian and white cowboys on this ranch. A big ruckus came up. Can't remember what started it all, but an Indian and a white got to arguing and then everybody was siding up for a fight—white against Indians. Me, I was in the middle. Didn't know which side to take 'cause I had friends in both camps.

"I thought I'd stay out of it, but before I knew it, I was in it. The first guy who swung at me was a white man so I hit back and was helping the Indians. I thumped away at my white friends, then in the confusion an Indian got me in the gut. Now that made me mad. Here I was on his side and he slugged me. What a battle! I ended up getting whopped by both sides and never did make up my mind about which side I belonged to."

We laughed, and I had a picture in my mind of Grandpa swinging at an Indian and a cowboy at the same time. Grandpa got up and put another log on the dying fire, so I knew he wasn't ready for bed.

"Do you miss your horse, Grandpa?" I asked, because thinking about cowboys and Indians just naturally made me think of horses.

"I don't miss the last one I had," Grandpa said. "I didn't ride much after my knees stiffened up, and he ate more than he was worth. But I still miss my Nelly horse."

"When did you have a horse named Nelly?"

"Oh, a long time ago. Nelly was the first horse I ever owned. She was a black-and-white pinto mare and the best bulldogging pony on the reservation. She was such a good horse that lots of cowboys wanted to buy her, but I wouldn't part with her no matter what they offered."

Grandpa poked at the fire with a stick and when it flared again I asked, "You said Nelly was a good calf-roping and bulldogging horse. When did you do those things?"

"In rodeos," he answered.

"You mean like Frontier Days in White River?"

"Well, not like the way Frontier Days is now," Grandpa said. "But the way it was six-some years ago when the rodeo first started.

"I must've been fourteen or fifteen when the first rodeo was held in White River. A bunch of ranchers and cowboys got together, hauled in some tough stock, built a corral, and started a yearly rodeo.

"In those early days there never used to be professional cowboys coming in to compete for prize money. Just us ordinary wranglers did the show. It was at one of those early rodeos that Nelly did me proud in bulldogging. She just took natural to riding close to a steer—never shied off. I could get right on top of the critter's horns and get a good hold. "'Course," he chuckled, "then it was up to me to throw 'em—I was pretty lightweight then and more often the steer get away 'fore I could throw 'em.

"But Nelly helped me win calf-roping events. She was good at sticking right at the dogies' heels—not too close—but near enough for me to toss a lasso over its head. Then Nell'd brake. She'd keep the rope taut while I jumped off to grab the calf. She kept that rope, which was fastened to the saddle, just tight enough around the calf's neck so that I could throw the critter and tie it up real quick. Nelly helped me pick up a lot of prize money."

"What else did you do during the celebration?" I asked.

"I was an Indian," Grandpa said, as he laughed and then explained. "My folks and me camped with the other Indians that came from all over the reservation for a visiting, feasting, and dancing get-together that was separate from the whites' affair. Every morning of the three-day celebration, the young men would get all fancied up in feathers and paint like in the old days when they'd go to war. 'Course we youngsters never had no chance to know how it was to fight in the old way—so we'd try to make up for it at Frontier Days.

"I recall the first time I took part. I was a funny lookin' Indian," he laughed, "and the other guys made fun of me. My face, hands, and arms were brown from being out in the sun and weather, but the rest of me was a lot paler—not as light as most whites but enough to show up in a bunch of full-bloods. My mom got embarrassed for me and went running to all the female relatives in the camp. They had a confab and came up with a concoction to color me."

"They dyed you?"

"That's right," Grandpa laughed. "It was important to Indian women to be proud of the men—especially the warriors. And even though I wasn't really going to war, they wanted me to look my best. Also, anything that caused embarrassment or shame to me was kinda a reflection on my whole family.

"So all those women yanked me into a tent and rubbed this stuff all over me. They used coffee, tobacco, and what I suspected was molasses—though they said it wasn't.

"When they were finally satisfied with my looks they escorted me a-singing and a-trilling those high notes that Indian women used to send their men off to war. I felt proud and happy when I mounted Nelly—bareback of course. I rode off with the other young men to attack the town of White River.

"We rode up from the river real quiet until we got to Main Street. It was just after sunrise and still cool, but as it warmed up I started attracting flies, and I was sure those women had put molasses in that dye.

"I didn't have time to worry about it because the warriors in the lead started whooping and galloping down the street. We fired our guns in the air, and it sounded like a real attack.

"We rode full speed up and down the street a couple of times and then discovered this covered wagon rolling along—'course this was all planned ahead of time. We surrounded the wagon, grabbed the driver, and scalped him. The driver and the Indians who scalped him got all bloody—'course it was only catsup, but it looked real. Then the most fun part began.

"The whites came charging at us to defend the town. This was the exciting and rough part of the show. Some of the young Indians and white cowboys had personal grudges that they settled in the fake fight. Real blood got spilled.

"There was always the temptation to really give it to those whites. But always at the right time before it could turn real, the leaders—a white and an Indian—gave a signal and we'd retreat to the river with the whites in pursuit. They'd won again."

I stared at the fire, not sure what to think. Grandpa had started out telling what I thought was going to be a funny story, but now at the end he sounded bitter and looked sad. I felt all mixed up and there was a lump in my throat.

The last bit of log fell into the ashes and I jumped away from the flying sparks. "Grandpa," I quietly asked, "how come when you talk about the past, you say you were a cowboy and an Indian?"

I sensed the regret in his short laugh when he answered, "'Cause I was both and both ways are gone forever."

"What are you now?"

"A tired old man," he said, and stiffly rose from his chair. "Make sure the fire's out before you come to bed." He walked to the house.

That was the last fire and those were the last stories Grandpa told. He died in the winter. I cried like a little kid because I loved him and missed him, and also because there would no longer be anybody to tell how it was to be a cowboy and an Indian.

Two

Long Ago

The First Christmas

The Moon When Horns Are Broken Off, Violet learned, was the month of December. No matter which name she used—Lakota or English—it was a cold time of year.

She remembered how it had been at home when she, Ina, Hokṡila, and Waṡtewin had spent the whole day on the worn buffalo robe huddled under the agency blankets. Unci and Tunkṡi did the same.

Ina and Tunkṡi had taken turns dashing to the small iron stove, tossing in logs, and then rushing back to the bed's warmth.

When the girls had to pee, they ran out to the side of the cabin away from the wind. When they hurriedly fled the bitter gale and crawled under the blankets, Unci had given each of the girls' pinches of *waṡna*. The grown-ups had only melted snow.

She had been so hungry. Violet had tried to pay no mind to her stomach, which cramped and growled for more. But the thin aroma of boiling beef made Violet's mouth water.

Unci had filled her iron kettle with snow, then added a few strips of dried meat, a handful of hard *tipsila,* and let the broth simmer all day.

She felt a pang of jealousy when baby Hokśila sucked at Ina's breast and guilty pleasure when he sobbed with rage because there was not enough to satisfy his hunger.

Finally, in dark evening, after the wind had died and the cabin could retain the stove's warmth, Unci gave them each a cup of the soup.

"I hope they have more to eat." Violet wished now that she and her sister, Waśtewin, were at boarding school. The agent had threatened to stop the High Bears' rations if the girls did not go to school.

Violet sighed. Ina, Unci, and Tunkśi would be pleased that the girls had plenty to eat, even though there were days in which the school wasn't much warmer than the High Bears' log house.

Violet moved calmly through the cold days but sensed strange expectant undercurrents gripping the school. The students seemed uneasy and restless. The teachers in the classroom and in the dorms, the cooks in the kitchen, the janitors, and the dairyman were talking about Christmas and wondering how it was going to be here in this godforsaken country.

The girls who worked in the kitchen reported that they'd been set to work making thirty-eight pumpkin pies with sugar and that they had used most of the milk so that there was none for breakfast. A fact that did not distress the children, for they didn't like milk. The pies were for Christmas dinner.

The big boys who worked in the dairy and helped shovel snow had unloaded barrels of apples from the freight wagon. They would be the children's Christmas gifts.

All of the talk of Christmas, the anticipated treat of pumpkin pie with sugar and not molasses, and the apples they all loved indicated to the children that Christmas was a day more special than any other. But then, why was Christmas to start tonight with a service in Mr. Burt's chapel at the agency?

But these wonderings were not voiced aloud, only in whispered Dakota conversations when a teacher wasn't near.

Now the children were silent, marching from the school to the chapel. Snow crunched beneath the hard-soled shoes they still hated even though their first blisters had healed. It was odd to be going to church at night. Some of the bigger boys spoke of slipping away in the dark, but they knew the bright starlight would have given them away. So they followed the little students and girls to the church.

Amber streams of light flowed from the windows of the small frame building, and the march quickened toward the beckoning warmth. As the first student stepped onto the porch, the door opened and Mr. Burt, wearing his white robe, helped the little ones into the church.

Eyes blinked in the yellow glow of kerosene lamps hanging from the ceiling, the oily smoke sharp in cold nostrils.

The youngest boys and girls walked to the front with their teacher; the girls filed in behind them. The men and boys sat on the other side with the biggest in the rear near the potbellied stove. It was the warmest place in the church but not the most comfortable, for it was soon too hot. But it was their duty to keep the fire going during the service.

Not a child uttered a word, but bright eyes gazed at the transformation of the plain sanctuary. Swags of green cedar boughs were draped over each window, above the altar, and on the organ where Mrs. Burt, smiling a welcome at the little ones, began a carol all of the students had practiced.

They stood as they had been trained and sang, then knelt as Mr. Burt prayed in Dakota. Next they sat as he stood beside the lectern and told the Christmas story.

The birth of a baby was common to the children; it was a natural event in their homes, but the idea of the baby's parents being turned away from shelter was foreign to a people who were always welcomed in any village.

Mr. Burt spoke of wise men coming to see the baby, and this the students also understood. A birth of a baby was a joyous time, and the elders—the wise men of the band—would especially welcome the birth because it meant the survival of the tribe.

The door creaked and a draft of cold darted over their ankles, but none of the well-trained children looked until they heard the soft shuffle of moccasins.

Now heads turned, but the children's excitement wasn't apparent as their young eyes followed three Indian men moving up the aisle. The first was the aged Drifting Goose, still starkly erect for his years, who majestically led two other elders. All wore wool robes draped over their shoulders; behind them their blanket-wrapped women aligned themselves in back of the stove.

Mr. Burt stopped speaking as the chief neared the lectern. He stepped forward as the men came to him, and he shook hands with each.

The teacher of the little ones nervously fluttered up from the front pew, pulling children off the pew and onto the floor, but Drifting Goose held up his hand and shook his head; he and his men sat at Mr. Burt's feet. Settled, he nodded at Mr. Burt, who resumed the story.

The minister spoke of shepherds watching their sheep in the cold night. "Shepherds" and "sheep"? The children silently wondered what they were and what was an angel? Was this sighting like a vision quest when young men went out alone to seek a spirit helper?

The sermon ended. Readily, the children rose and sang "O Little Town of Bethlehem," which they had practiced and memorized without grasping its meaning. But, suddenly, as Violet sang, the words and the meaning came together in her mind and she understood that the students were singing the story Mr. Burt had told.

Seated again, the students watched Mr. Burt prepare the bread and wine at the altar and wondered why their teachers knelt so humbly at the rail, eating the bread and sipping the wine. They quietly marveled that Drifting Goose and his party also knelt at the Communion rail. At home Violet knew adults who had become Christian, and she assumed that the Driving Goose band must have also converted to this new religion.

"Mmmmooo," quietly sounded from outdoors, and the boys by the windows stared into the dark night.

"Moooo," louder. Then the bass of men's voices rumbled over creaking leather, and again a dart of cold air swirled about the children's ankles as the door creaked open. This time feet stomped and spurs jangled as two booted cowboys came into the church. They took off their hats, nodded to Mr. Burt, and opened their long canvas mackinaws to the warmth of the stove. None of the children stirred, but they knew of these white men who trailed cattle to reservations—maybe to theirs.

The organ wheezed as Mrs. Burt pumped and began the final carol. The cowboys pulled out their sacks of tobacco and papers and rolled a smoke as the children sang, "O Come All Ye Faithful."

Drifting Goose and his elders stood. From under his blanket the chief pulled out his pipe bag and then walked to the stove. He tamped *knikinic* into the red stone bowl, and one of the cowboys struck a match. The old chief drew on the pipe and offered it to the sky, the earth, and to the four directions before he smoked and shared the pipe with his men and the cowboys.

The singing stopped; the cowboys, warm and rested, left the church, raising a hand in thanks to Mr. Burt. Leather creaked as they mounted their horses and followed the herd.

Drifting Goose wrapped his blanket securely about his tall form, lifted a hand sign of peace and farewell to Mr. Burt, and led his men and women into the night.

The boarding-school students filed out into the dark and cold. The big boys carried sleeping little ones and led the way back to the school. Bright stars lit their way; snow crunched underfoot, cows mooed in the distance, and the deep voice of an Indian man commanded the horses pulling the wagon that carried Drifting Goose to his home near the river.

Violet listened to the harness bells until they jingled away to silence.

Fool Soldiers

It was the time the Teton called Moon When Winter Sets In, the time the white men called November 1862. The elders and women gloried in the peaceful days and felt sympathy for their relatives, the Santee, who were at war with the whites in Minnesota, but the young men were restless. There was no need to hunt or to steal more horses. There was no opportunity to make war, to count coup, or to show their courage and fully become men.

Waanatan, Charger, and his brother-friend, Kills-and-Comes, were among the restless ones. They had returned successful from their vision quest and now had the respect of the tribe, but their valor was unproven. The revelation from Wakantanka had been similar for both young men, and, as a result, both had made a vow to rescue white captives.

The Two-Kettles thought that the young men had made a rash promise, for the tribe was neutral in the Santee war and would not interfere with anything their relatives did. As the weeks went by, many forgot what the young men had vowed to do, but the villagers saw that where Charger led, Kills-and-Comes followed and that Swift Bear was often with them.

Every day the three friends went to Primeau's store, a temporary trading post the Frenchman had built above the abandoned Fort La Fromboise and old Fort Pierre on the Missouri River. The place was still called Fort Pierre by some Indians and whites, but the Frenchman and his friends named the trading post Fort Primeau.

The trader, Primeau, encouraged Charger and Kills-and-Comes to rescue white captives and promised to report any news that came his way. But when months passed and there was no word of Santee captives, Primeau and the young men began to think that perhaps the Santee would not venture so far to the west of their Minnesota home.

Still the young men went to Primeau's. Their visits were a welcome change from the quiet monotony of the Two-Kettles' village. So it was that one morning, the three friends were lounging in the store when a runner came from the river bottom to announce the arrival of Major Galpin, his Yankton wife, and a party of miners. They had come to rest a while and exchange news with Primeau before continuing their journey down the Missouri.

Galpin told Primeau of his party's encounter with the Santee band, which his Indian wife had correctly identified as hostile. "My woman was suspicious," said Galpin, "when the Indians said they were peaceful hunters. She knew that the Lakota don't take old men hunting."

Major Galpin went on to tell of the ambush the Santee had

Long Ago

set, their narrow escape, and, most important to Charger, of the white woman who had called for help from the shore.

"She was a ragged wretch," Galpin reported, "but before any of the Indians stopped her, she yelled that a Mrs. Duley, Mrs. Wright, and six white children were prisoners in the Santee camp."

Charger was elated. At last his vision could be fulfilled. "I will go to rescue the white captives!" he shouted joyfully.

Kills-and-Comes and Swift Bear added their eager agreement, but Primeau laughed at the zealousness of the young men. "It will take more than just the three of you to rescue the prisoners. The Santee won't let the captives go easily. They'll put up a fight!"

"That's right," Galpin put in. "They seemed desperate to me. Undoubtedly, they've been hounded all the way from Minnesota."

"We will enlist others like ourselves to help us," Charger answered. "There are many Teton young men who long to do a brave deed. Come," he said to his friends, "we have much to do."

Charger kicked and whipped his horse into a gallop as they neared the village. "*Hoka Hey!*" the three shouted, riding furiously through the camp.

The people scattered out of the way. Voices were raised in alarm, and startled warriors ran for their weapons.

At the far end of the camp circle, the young men jerked their horses into sharp, rearing turns. They sprinted back to the center, flaunting their skill on the wild-eyed animals. They ended the mad ride with a flourish as they reined their snorting, mouth-foamed horses to an abrupt halt.

Children, young men, and giggling, excited maidens cheered their horsemanship. Older men and women scolded them for abusing the animals. The warriors denounced them for raising a false alarm.

"Brothers!" Charger shouted over the clamor as he, Kills-and-Comes, and Swift Bear danced their horses in tight circles, "the time has come to show your courage! Join us! We go to rescue white captives from the Santee."

"*Wacintonśni*, fools!" called a warrior who turned his back and stomped disgustedly back to his tipi.

Many of the people moved away, muttering and shaking their heads at the rash boys. But here and there were young men who chafed at their inactivity and longed to prove their bravery.

"I will go," one cried. "And I," called out another and another, until there were eight standing before Charger.

"Ho!" Charger exulted, sweeping his arm over the eager youths. We will be soldiers against the Santee!"

"*Akicita wacintonśni,* Fool Soldiers!" an older warrior scornfully yelled.

Others picked up the name, and soon a crowd followed the young men, laughing and chanting, "Fool soldiers, Fool Soldiers."

Charger ignored the derisive taunts and led his followers to a secluded spot along the river where they could make their plans.

"We are young," Charger began his harangue, "none of us have counted coup. We have no knowledge of battle save what our uncles and grandfathers have told us. Our journey to find the captives may be long and cold, for already the north wind has sent a snow warning. When we find the Santee we must be wily. Speak wisely and avoid bloodshed in which the captives might be harmed. But, if we must fight, we will do so bravely and be prepared to die!"

"*Han!* Ho!" shouted the young men. "We are not afraid to die!"

"You have heard," Charger went on, waving his hand toward the village, "what our people have called us—'crazy' and 'fools'—and," his voice lowered, "some will call us traitors because we dare to think of going to the aid of the whites.

"We will be ridiculed, perhaps even exiled, for what we plan to do. Are you strong enough to bear that?"

Again the young men shouted. "We are strong! We are not afraid!"

"*Waśte,* good!" Charger was pleased. "Go now and prepare yourselves for the journey. Pack food and extra blankets. When all is ready gather at Primeau's, where I will be bartering buffalo robes for coffee and sugar."

The young men scattered.

Primeau gave Charger full value and more for the robes, for the Frenchman knew it would be necessary that the band of young men hold a feast for the Santee before any bargaining for the captives took place.

"After you rescue the captives," Primeau told Charger, "bring them to me. I will care for them until a way is found to take them to Fort Randall."

He followed the youth out of the post to where the others were waiting. "Good luck!" he cried after the eleven young men who rode off, whooping and making their ponies prance to the fording place on the river's bottom.

The young men, eager for adventure, swam their horses across the river and started north for the Santee camp. They rode steadily until twilight and made camp for the night even though they were not tired. They wanted to keep the horses fresh, for they would be needed for barter as well as transportation on the return trip with the captives.

In midmorning of the second day away from their village,

the Fool Soldiers, as they laughingly called themselves, came upon the camp of Bone Necklace, chief of a band of Yanktonais, on the Swan Lake Creek. The Yanktonais made the young men welcome.

Charger told them of his intent and inquired among Bone Necklace's people for news of the captives. Some of the Yankton warriors had come across the Santee band on a hunt.

"The Santee are led by White Lodge," the warriors said. "He has eighty tipis and is moving downstream to seek help from the Teton. There are many crying children in the Santee camp. They are hungry and destitute. This is why White Lodge attempted to capture the Galpin boat. He did not wish to kill them; he wanted the boat's provisions."

The Fool Soldiers rode about fifteen miles up the Missouri and found White Lodge's band setting up camp for the night. Near the Santee, but not among them, the Fool Soldiers pitched the one tipi they had brought for shelter.

Charger left his followers to prepare a feast of coffee, sugar, and hard bread, and he walked alone to invite the Santee to eat.

White Lodge greeted the young man in a cordial yet reserved manner. He accepted Charger's invitation to eat, and soon the most of the village but those too ill too walk came to the Fool Soldiers' camp. They drank the sweetened coffee, which they had not had since leaving Minnesota, and wolfed down the chunks of bread. Many parents gave their portion to their children. Charger was dismayed at the hunger he saw in the little ones' faces. He also noticed that there were none of the white captives in the group.

After White Lodge had eaten, Charger told the chief of his mission and requested a formal meeting with the Santee council.

"I do not bargain with boys," White Lodge declared scornfully.

"We have horses to trade," Charger said loudly and the Santee heard and pressed their chief to call the council.

Reluctantly White Lodge agreed, and soon the council was seated around the warmth of the Fool Soldiers' fire. Charger produced a pipe, lit it with the proper ceremony, and passed it first, as a sign of honor, to White Lodge. After the pipe made its rounds of the council, the Fool Soldiers replenished the tin cups with coffee, and Charger spoke.

"Welcome, our cousins, the Santee," he greeted. "Our hearts are glad to see you in our land. We hold only good feelings for you. You see us here," Charger said, waving his hand to his followers and back to himself, "We are only young men, as White Lodge has said. None of us have counted coup or seen battle. We know this. Our people call us crazy and fools. But we are brave in our hearts and want to do something good."

Charger paused, summoning the best words to impress the Santee. "If," he went on, "a man owns a thing he likes, he will not part with it for nothing. We have come here to buy the white captives from you and give them back to their friends."

A murmur of astonishment at the young man's words went among the Santee, and Charger quickly added, "We will give our own good horses for the captives. Our ponies are the best of the Two-Kettles' herd, the swiftest and strongest of all Teton horses. We will trade horses for the captives."

Again a murmur from the Santee, but this time it was a favorable sound. Charger sat and stared into the fire. His heart beat rapidly and his hands were wet with the sweat of relief now that he had spoken. But what would the Santee do? He dared not show disrespect and look at White Lodge, who sat in an ominous silence.

The chief slowly drank his coffee and ignored the arguments

of his men. The young Fool Soldiers tried to sit stolidly serious, as befitted the moment. They knew that any impatient movement would be detrimental to their cause. White Lodge rose.

He arranged his blanket in dignified folds about his old body and stood, a stately, awesome figure, silhouetted against the fire. "We come from the east," the old chief began, "where the sky is red from the fires which burn the homes of whites who built on Santee land. The ground is red with the blood of whites the Santee have killed. The captives we have taken after the killing of many people. We can never again be friends with the whites for we have done many things that they think are bad.

"But we say," he shouted angrily, "that we have not done as much bad as the whites have done to us! We will not give up the captives!" White Lodge declared fiercely. "We will fight until we are dead!"

The old chief sat and his council spoke loudly among itself, some agreeing and others disagreeing with his words, but none rose. Charger motioned for Kills-and-Comes to speak.

"Our horses are the fastest of all the Tetons," Kills-and-Comes bragged. "We will trade them for the white captives and they will carry you speedily and safely into battle."

The Fool Soldiers nodded in assent as Kills-and-Comes sat, and there was talk among the Santee. Charger waited for another of White Lodge's men to speak aloud, and when none rose he motioned to Swift Bear.

"Our horses are the strongest of all of the Tetons," Swift Bear cried. They will carry you far without tiring. We offer them in exchange for the captives."

White Lodge rose to still the loud argument among his council. "No!" he shouted. "We will not give up the captives!"

In the silence that followed, Charger rose and spoke grimly.

"Three times," he said, "we have offered our horses for the captives. You have refused. Now," he said taking a step toward the Santee camp, "we will take the captives. We will put them on our horses. If you make trouble for us, the soldiers with guns will come against you from the east," he shouted and pointed. "And the Teton will come against you from the west," he pointed across the river. "Then we shall see if you are brave!"

The Fool Soldiers jumped to their feet, menacingly brandishing their guns and whooping war cries. The older Santee rose more slowly and began to move toward their camp and the protection of their warriors, who waited in the background.

Before they could move far, a voice rose out of the darkness from the group of men who did not sit in council.

"Father." The elders turned and looked at Black Hawk, the son of their chief. He hesitated and then stepped in front of White Lodge.

"I have love and respect for you and the others who are old, but," and he turned to the Fool Soldiers, "I also have respect for these young men who have shown great courage in daring to speak in such a manner to us.

"You have done right," Black Hawk said to Charger. "We have eaten your food, and it was good. You are straight, brave young men, respected among your own people or they would not have let you come." He paused and turned sad eyes upon White Lodge.

"My father, we are starving. We need the strong, swift horses of the Teton so that we may hunt. We need the brave horses of the Teton to go to live in Canada, for we can never return to Minnesota. I have one white child in my lodge which I will give up even though my wife will grieve." He turned to face the other Santee. "Let you do as I have done and give up the captives!"

The Santee council huddled in conference. Their younger men shouted agreement with Black Hawk, for they wanted the Teton horses. White Lodge turned and headed back to the Santee camp; the council followed. Black Hawk came to Charger.

"We will exchange the captives for the horses," the chief's son said. "Wait here while we prepare our women and persuade those who have adopted the three little girls to give them up. The white girls replaced Santee children who died and it will be like death again in the lodges of the mothers. We will send word when we are ready." Black Hawk walked away.

The Fool Soldiers took down their tipi and prepared to move quickly with the captives as soon as the exchange was made. The sky was black with low snow clouds that covered the night-lights of the heavens. The Fool Soldiers huddled around their dying fire, blankets tightly wrapped against the chill wind that howled across the river. They waited. Gradually most of the young men curled up to sleep on the cold ground. Charger and Kills-and-Comes watched.

Charger was worried. "They are so long. Something must have gone wrong in the Santee camp."

"White Lodge has probably changed his mind again," Kills-and-Comes said, "but do not worry. The warriors want our horses. They will force the old man to trade."

The night was turning to the grayness that preceded dawn when the Fool Soldiers were summoned.

Charger woke his young men, and they caught the horses that had been hobbled nearby. They followed the Santee messenger to a large tipi in the center of the camp. Here was where the exchange would be made. The Fool Soldiers tethered the horses near the entrance and left a guard to watch the animals, lest the desperate Santee steal them. The rest of the young men entered the tipi with Charger.

A fire burned in the center of the lodge. Black Hawk, who sat across from the entrance, motioned for the Fool Soldiers to seat themselves on his left. On the other side of the tipi they saw one white woman with six children huddled about her.

Pity filled Charger's heart as he looked at the captives. The whites were poorly clothed, almost naked except for ragged cotton garments. Charger was struck by the vacant stare of the woman. She seemed unaware of her surroundings and made no effort to comfort the whimpering younger children. Two girls were at her sides, supporting her. One of them, the oldest of the children, bent to murmur to the little boy who snuggled closer to her. She comforted the boy and shushed the frightened wails of the other children. Then she proudly lifted her head and stared curiously at Charger and his followers.

Black Hawk spoke, "This is the woman Martha Duley, and the two girls at her side are hers. The woman is mad," he said in disgust. "The other three girls have no mother. They were adopted by our women." His gaze moved to a grief-stricken Santee woman, her face blackened and her hair hanging in ragged strands over her face. Black Hawk's face softened with pity and Charger guessed that the woman was his wife, but the chief's son went on.

"The boy belongs to the other white woman, Wright, and lived in the lodge of my father."

"Where is the Wright woman?" Charger asked.

Black Hawk shook his head. "My father has changed his mind

about parting with her, but he will let the boy go for one horse and a blanket."

Charger was dismayed. He knew now that the Santee had changed their minds about a wholesale exchange of captives for the horses. He would have to bargain for each captive individually.

Wearily he nodded, and Black Hawk motioned for his wife to bring the Wright boy. The child was almost asleep, leaning against the girl who held him with her good arm. She gave the boy a little shake as the Indian woman approached. The boy cowered against the girl and Charger heard him cry, "Mama?" The girl bent her head and whispered encouragingly. The boy looked questioningly at her, and when she nodded with a smile he got up and let the woman lead him to Charger.

Charger handed her a blanket and gently took the small boy's hand. "*Hau, hokśila,*" he greeted and then realized that he should have spoken English. But, to his surprise, the child responded gravely, "*Hau,* Waanatan."

Charger looked at Black Hawk, who was smiling. "The boy has been treated as a son in my father's lodge. He knows the language and manners of a Dakota boy and has been told your name."

The boy sat quietly beside Kills-and-Comes as Charger continued the bargaining. On and on he bartered through the day. Each captive, starting with the youngest child, went for a horse and blanket, or coffee and sugar. Finally, the oldest girl moved to the Fool Soldiers' side, and when her mother was traded she spoke to Charger in halting Dakota.

"Waanatan, my mother is lame and will need my help to walk across the tipi."

Charger looked at the girl who seemed so much older than the twelve winters he had been told she was. "Cannot the Santee woman help her?" he asked, afraid that if Sarah was allowed on the other side the Santee might not let her return.

Black Hawk spoke, "My woman does not want to touch the madwoman. Let the girl help her mother."

Charger understood the Santee aversion to insanity, but he was still reluctant to let the girl go. "What is your name?" he asked the girl as he tried to think what to do.

"Sarah Duley," she answered. "But the Santee have called me Shining Hair."

Charger nodded. The Santee had named her well, even though the smoke of lodge fires had darkened the fair hair. "Cannot your mother walk alone?" he asked.

Sarah shook her head. "No, she has a crippled foot and has no crutch." Her eyes filled with tears as she added, "And she must be led because she—she . . . ," the girl faltered and looked away so that Charger would not see her weep.

Charger was overwhelmed with pity for the girl, sensing that she must have suffered terribly during captivity and that her mother had been an additional burden. "Go," he said to her.

Sarah moved to her mother's side and with her good arm touched the woman gently on the shoulder as if, Charger thought, the girl were the mother and the mother were the child. Charger saw that the woman was badly crippled as she limped across the tipi, leaning heavily on Sarah. Inwardly, he groaned. It would be difficult traveling with the maimed captive. He should have tried to strike a better bargain for the handicapped woman.

All the Fool Soldiers had left was one horse and four guns, and Mrs. Wright still had not been seen. White Lodge entered the tipi carrying his war club and looked with disgust at the young Tetons. "Go, he commanded. "You have the captives!"

But Charger did not move. "There is still the Wright woman."

"No," White Lodge growled. "She is my wife. I am old; my first wife is old. I need the white woman in my lodge. She takes good care of me. I will not let her go!"

The Fool Soldiers exclaimed angrily and demanded that the chief release the white woman. Charger jumped to his feet. He was furious. "The Santee are liars!" he shouted. "They promised to exchange all of the captives for the horses. Instead they have taken much more. Now White Lodge breaks his word even more by denying us the last captive!"

White Lodge rushed toward the captives, his war club raised. "I will kill them all!" he stormed.

The children screamed and clung to Sarah. The Fool Soldiers jumped in front of the captives to ward off White Lodge's swinging club. Black Hawk moved swiftly and caught his father's arm before the club struck.

"Black Hawk is wise!" Charger shouted above the uproar of crying children and yelling Santee. Black Hawk forcibly seated the chief. The old man breathed heavily and glared at Charger.

"The Santee forget," Charger spoke firmly, "that if you harm the captives, soldiers with many guns will give you no rest. They will pursue until you are all dead. Remember, too, that the Teton will also come against you."

Charger's heart pounded after he had spoken. He held his breath, waiting to see if the Santee believed him, for he knew that his threat was meaningless. It would be a long time before soldiers heard of the captives, and the Santee could easily escape into the prairie wilderness. Nor could Charger count on the Teton coming to his aid. Yet the destitute Santee did not know Charger was bluffing.

The Santee gathered around White Lodge. He listened to their arguments and, at last, in sullen silence, nodded. Black

Hawk signaled to his wife; she ran from the tipi to get the Wright woman.

"I will take a horse, a gun, and two blankets for the woman," White Lodge bargained.

"No!" Charger answered shortly. "We will give you one horse and two blankets. No more!"

White Lodge moved to rise but was restrained by Black Hawk. Reluctantly the old man agreed to the counteroffer.

Charger stood and motioned to his followers to take the woman and children out. Sarah understood the need to get away from the Santee as quickly as possible and urged the children to go with the Fool Soldiers, while she grasped her mother's arm and led her after the others.

Charger waited alone until Julia Wright was brought into the tipi. Again his heart was filled with pity as he saw the woman's face. It was still bruised and swollen from White Lodge's anger of four days before when she had alerted Galpin of the presence of the captives in the Santee camp. She stared uncomprehendingly at Charger when he took her arm to guide her out of the tipi. "Come," he said in English, "you are free."

Outside, Charger held onto the woman's arm as he followed the Fool Soldiers, who were carrying the younger children and hurrying the others forward. It was evening time again. They had been in the Santee camp for twenty-four hours and had eaten nothing since they feasted the Santee. Charger and Kills-and-Comes were weary from lack of sleep, but the party had to get as faraway from the village as they could before night fell.

They were only a short distance from the Santee camp when Charger knew they had to stop. The wind that had been threatening snow for the past two days at last brought a blizzard.

The small tipi was set up, and everyone, except the Fool Soldier who would stand guard, crowded in. The three blankets that remained were given to the captives, who fell immediately into exhausted sleep.

Charger was worried. He expected White Lodge to follow and try to retrieve the captives. The Fool Soldiers had only four guns for protection. All of the horses were gone and they had no food. They were more than one hundred miles from Primeau's post and the Two-Kettles' village. "Would he be able to get the captives safely there?" Charger wondered before he fell into a fitful rest.

It was still dark when the guard woke Charger. He roused the others, and in minutes the party was moving down along the riverbank through cold, swirling snow. Charger noticed that the Wright woman walked more and more slowly until she was some distance behind. The girl, Sarah, had been following her mother, who was supported by Swift Bear. Now, Sarah turned and waited for Julia.

Charger waited until the woman and the girl came up to him. "You must keep up," he said to Julia, who nodded mutely.

"She has no shoes," Sarah told him, knowing that Julia would not say why she moved so slowly.

In his eagerness to get away from the Santee, Charger had not noticed the white woman's lack of footgear. He called for a brief rest and apologized to Julia. "I am sorry that I did not see your bare feet," he said, sitting in the snow and removing his moccasins.

"You must have covering for your feet or they will freeze." Julia looked unbelievingly at him as he handed her his moccasins.

"You cannot walk in cold snow," Charger said, urging the moccasins on her. "Put them on."

"But what will you wear?" Julia protested.

Charger smiled. "I will wrap strips of blanket around my feet." He ripped the cloth as he spoke. "Do not worry. A Teton's feet are tough like leather."

"How can I ever thank you?" Julia said as she tied the moccasins. "Not only for the moccasins, but for rescuing us. I was afraid White Lodge would kill us all. He was so angry after I called to the people in the boat. I had given up all hope of ever being released from captivity."

"It was the people in the boat who told us how to find you," Charger explained. He stood and motioned the party on.

"Aren't you all young to be doing a man's . . ." Sarah broke off, not wanting to insult Charger. "I mean, among the Santee all of the warriors were old."

"The Teton become men at an early age," Charger answered. "And they must show their courage by doing a man's brave deed."

"Is that why you came to rescue us?"

Charger nodded. "That was part of it. We had heard of the Santee war long moons ago, and our hearts were sad that the Santee had taken white women and children captives. I vowed to rescue white captives if ever I had the chance."

This Indian amazed Sarah. "How did you learn to speak English?"

"I visited with every white man who came on the river," Charger said. "I learned your language easily and even know some French from Primeau, the trader whose store is near my village. My people, the Two Kettles, say that I learned English and understand the white people because I am part white." He looked at Sarah to see if she believed him. "My grandfather was one of the first Americans to visit our tribe."

"Who was that?" Sarah asked.

"He was called Lewis."

"Do you mean the explorer?"

"Do you know of him?"

"Yes," Sarah nodded. She did not know what to say to his claim, which seemed to be important to him. She trudged along quietly for a while. Then she asked, "Do all of your people feel kindness toward white people?"

"No," Charger shook his head sadly. "Many of my people call me and my followers crazy, and even traitors, for going to the rescue of whites. We are known as the Fool Soldiers, but we are not ashamed of the name. Is it foolish to do a good thing?"

Sarah shook her head and said. "We don't hate the Santee either—they treated us children as if we were their own. The old woman, Anna, who lived with us in her son's tipi, cared for Nancy and me as if we her own grandchildren. She dressed mother's wound and mine—she . . . ," Sarah's voice broke and her eyes brightened with tears, "loved Nancy and me. When she knew that we were going to leave with you, she cut her hair, blackened her face, and mourned as if we had died."

Charger's heart was stirred by the girl's compassion for her captors. He knew that her feelings for Indians were unacceptable to most white people. He thought her people would consider her as foolish as he was considered by the Two Kettles. Charger felt a bond between himself and the white girl.

When the rescue party reached the Bone Necklace camp, Charger gratefully accepted the Yanktonais' offer to spend the night. He and his friends were weary after the twenty-four-hour parley with the Santee, and the weakened captives were exhausted.

The next morning Bone Necklace gave the Fool Soldiers an old cart he had found along the river. All of the children could now ride, and the band could move faster. The chief also gave them extra blankets and food to last until they reached Primeau's post.

Martha could not ride on the horse because of the cart's shafts lashed to its sides, and when she was placed in the cart with the children, the load was too heavy for the animal. So Charger divided his young men into three groups to spell each other in pushing the cart to aid the horse.

The snow had stopped, and they made a long, cold march before Charger called a halt. They camped that night along the river in the spot the whites called Forest City because of the thick grove of trees that gave shelter from the harsh wind.

As the weak sun rose in the morning so did the Fool Soldiers and the captives. The younger children cried fretfully when they had to leave the warm tipi and get in the open cart. All of them were coughing and had runny noses. Julia told Charger that the two Ireland girls were feverish. Charger knew he would have to get them to Primeau's soon.

He picked a route away from the Missouri and up to the prairie where the traveling was easier, even if there was nothing to break the wind. The sun was high when he led them back to where the river widened at the fording place. But the shallow stream was covered with the first winter ice, and Charger knew the crossing would be difficult. Kills-and-Comes volunteered to test the ice and find the best way to cross.

Charger watched anxiously as his brother-friend walked on the firm ice near the shore. A little way out, however, he plunged through into shoulder-deep water. But Kills-and-Comes plodded on. On the opposite shore, as he came shivering out of the water, Primeau, who had watched daily for their return, met him. With the Frenchman's assistance, he stumbled out onto the sandy shore.

The trader summoned his friends Dupree and La Plante from the post. They carried Primeau's sturdy boat into the water and poled across the river, following the trail Kills-and-Comes had broken through the ice. It wasn't long before the captives and the Fool Soldiers were in the secure warmth of Primeau's post.

"You did it, Charger!" Primeau exulted as he bustled about preparing hot drink and food.

Once they were warm, the Fool Soldiers became restless and longed to go to their homes. "I deliver the captives safely to you," Charger said to Primeau. The trader nodded and answered, "I will give them food and clothing. They will rest for a few days, and then Dupree and La Plante will take them to Fort Randall and the soldiers."

Julia Wright shook Charger's hand. "We will never forget what you have done for us."

Charger nodded and moved toward the door to follow his young men who had already left. Sarah Duley ran to him, grabbed his hand, and kissed it. "Thank you," she sobbed.

Charger jerked his hand away as if it were burned. He looked down at the weeping white girl and his heart beat painfully fast, but he only nodded and walked away.

Three

Legends

Sun Gazer

Once there was a boy who was dearly loved by his mother and grandmother. He was the only male in the lodge, since his father had not returned from a battle with an enemy tribe.

The women had a difficult time without a hunter to provide meat or hides for clothing and tipi covers. True, their relatives shared with them, but they were the poorest lodge in the Lakota village. Thus the women treasured the boy and often spoke of how he would become a great hunter and their poverty would end.

The boy, as a babe, was always near his mother or grandmother and rarely cried. He was swaddled in a cradle-board with only his round face showing and from it he observed his small world. When it was time to prepare a meal over the open fire, the cradle-board was hung from a tipi pole indoors or from a tree outdoors. From this perch he was safe from the fire and could watch his mother and grandmother and the activities of the camp. He was content to have it so and enjoyed the gentle swaying of the cradle-board.

One spring morning he was so placed, when the sun burst over the hill and shone on his face. He blinked and cooed at the bright warmth and cried when the cradle-board was moved indoors. After that he fussed until his mother placed the cradle-board where he could watch the sun. On cloudy days he was unhappy.

The two women and their relatives laughed at the boy's desire to see the sun and called him Sun Gazer.

Soon Sun Gazer was toddling about the lodge and exploring the world outdoors. These new adventurers kept him amused, yet in the midst of his play he would pause, look up at the sky, and gaze at the sun.

And so it went until the tenth winter of Sun Gazer's life when he lay near to death, pale and shivering with a chill of an illness that the medicine man could not cure. Sun Gazer's mother and grandmother wept as they wrapped the boy in warm robes and tempted him to eat the rich soup of cracked buffalo bones. Still, Sun Gazer grew weaker and weaker.

Spring came, the time when Sun Gazer and other boys his age were to be with the males of the tribe to learn hunting skills they had only played at. But Sun Gazer, to weak to join the group, could only watch as he lay propped against a willow backrest where the sun's rays warmed him.

Day by day, Sun Gazer grew stronger, but from that time on he wanted only to stay in the sun. On cloudy days he was listless and pale, and each winter he weakened and pined until he was revived by the spring sun. His mother and grandmother despaired, knowing that the boy would never be a hunter even if he lived to be a man.

The boy's fourteenth winter was one of extreme cold and deep snow. By spring Sun Gazer was so weak that even with the women's support he couldn't walk to his backrest in the sun. At dawn he crawled to the spot and back into the lodge when the sun set. Again he was revived, but the long winter had taken its toll. He made no effort to strengthen his weak muscles but only gazed at the sun, following its passage across the sky until his eyelids could no longer close, even at night.

One sundown the boy did not return to the tipi, and the women found him groping about on his hands and knees trying to find his way. His wide-open eyes stared at nothing; he was blind from his constant gazing at the sun.

The women wept and carried him to their lodge. Then they called the medicine man, but all he could do was cool Sun Gazer's burning eyes with a soothing bath. Then he left, shaking his head sadly, "The sun has claimed him."

After that the women tried to keep Sun Gazer in the lodge, but he learned to find his way outdoors. Even though he could no longer see the sun, his face followed its warm rays through the day.

Again, on another evening, Sun Gazer did not return to the tipi.

His mother and grandmother went to the spot where he spent his days, but he was not there. The women alerted the village and a search began.

Soon Sun Gazer's lifeless body was found on a hill west of the camp where he had followed the last rays of the setting sun.

The whole village mourned with the boy's mother and grandmother who wailed and angrily cursed the sun for stealing the boy's spirit.

"Bury him where he died," they requested. "Do not put him

on a scaffold where the sun can take his body. Put him in the ground away from the sun!"

And so it was done.

Each day the grieving mother and grandmother visited Sun Gazer's grave. On the fourth day they found a small green shoot growing from the mound of dirt.

The next day it was taller, and so it grew, until one morning they found the plant had bloomed a single flower as golden as the sun. Its head faced the rising sun.

The amazed women called the people. The whole village watched golden flower's face follow the sun across the sky and saw it droop as the sun set.

Takoża Said "Goo"

There was once a man who was renowned among many tribes for his skill as a hunter and warrior. The people praised him so much that he became puffed up and boastful.

"Yes," he bragged, "I am such a great man that all creatures fear and obey me!"

The warrior's manner irritated the people, and they were shamed and embarrassed by his gloating airs. One wise old grandmother knew that it was not good for anyone to be so puffed with pride, and she decided the man needed a lesson.

"I know one who is greater than this mighty warrior," the old grandmother whispered among the people. "This one will not run away in fear nor will he do what the warrior says!"

Soon all of the people were whispering, and the warrior heard what they said. He rushed angrily to the old grandmother's lodge.

"Show me this person who will not run from me nor do what I say."

Grandmother, ignoring the warrior's rudeness, calmly motioned to the rear of her lodge where a baby boy sat on a buffalo robe playing with his gourd rattle.

"This is Takoża," she said, "one who is greater than you."

The warrior didn't know about babies since he spent most of his time hunting, fishing, going to war, and bragging about his exploits. So he was surprised at how small the baby was. As he looked at Takoża, he thought that it would be easy to get this small person to obey.

Takoża looked at the warrior, smiled, and said, "Goo." Then he stuck his thumb in his mouth.

"Goo?" the warrior repeated, not understanding Takoża's word.

Takoża popped his thumb from his mouth. "Goo," he repeated, smiling at the man.

"Hah!" the warrior yelled. "You dare to challenge me?" He took a threatening step forward. "Come here, Takoża!" he ordered.

"Goo?" Takoża seemed to question his eyes wide.

"Yes," yelled the warrior. "Now! Come here!"

"Goo," quivered Takoża, and a tear rolled down his cheek.

"Stop saying Goo and come to me!" The warrior shouted furiously, stomped his foot, and shook his fist in a fierce dance.

Takoża's mouth opened wide, but instead of saying, "Goo," he squenched his eyes tight and bawled and yelled.

"What?" asked the warrior in amazed alarm at the terrible noises Takoża made. He stopped dancing and stared at the baby.

When the warrior stopped yelling and stomping his feet, Takoża ceased his bawling. He looked wonderingly at the man, hiccuped, and said, "Goo." Then he put his thumb back in his mouth.

The warrior stumbled out of the lodge.

"Well, Warrior," the old grandmother asked, "did Takoża obey you?"

"No," the shamed warrior said. "Takoża is a fierce little person who makes the most frightful sounds. He is mightier than I."

Grandmother carried Takoża from the lodge. "Here, Warrior, hold Takoża." She held the baby to the man.

"No," the warrior stepped back in alarm. "He might start yelling."

"Are you afraid of this small one?" Grandmother asked, and the warrior, not wanting to be thought a coward, took Takoża in his arms.

The warrior and the baby, thumb in his mouth, carefully looked at each other. Takoża put his wet thumb on the man's face. The warrior flinched at its damp touch. Then he couldn't help but grin as the baby's little hand patted his chin.

"Goo," Takoża said, and smiled.

The Tribe of the Burnt Thigh

Many long years ago there were several different tribes of Indians who lived across the land. One group called themselves Lakota. Within this large Lakota nation were seven smaller tribes, and each had a special name because of something they did or something that happened to them.

It was in the time before the horse, and the people walked. A band of Lakota had been hunting for buffalo in the tallgrass country. The hunters had been lucky to find and kill many of the large beasts, and the women's buffalo-hide packs were heavy with meat. The older boys and girls watched over the pack dogs pulling the travois made from the poles and skins of the band's small tipis.

Each travois was loaded with bed robes and cooking utensils. These dogs were well trained but still could not be trusted to carry the precious meat.

The people were happy as they made their way home. The women chatted as they walked behind the children and dogs. The men, moving in long easy strides, were divided into four groups: those who walked in front of the band, those on the right of the women and children, those on the left, and those who guarded the rear. The men talked as they moved along, but all were alert to danger from the enemy Ojibwa or from a prairie fire.

The enemy tribe the men could fight without fear. But in this Moon When the Leaves Are Turning Brown, the grass could catch fire easily, and the flames could quickly spread. All that the people could do was try to stay out of its path.

The band was only one more day's walk from its main village on the shores of a clear lake. Waiting for them were the grandfathers and grandmothers and mothers with babies and very small children. How happy they would all be to see the hunting party return with meat and new hides—enough for the whole village!

The men walking far in advance of the main band had found a good campsite by a small nameless stream. They knew that the larger Big Sioux River was only a little way south, but the small stream would do for this last night away from home.

The sun was setting on their backs as the people reached the campsite. The women quickly hung their packs in the trees, where the dogs or wild animals could not reach them. The girls unpacked the dog travois and helped their mothers put up the tipis.

The boys took meat from a special pack to feed the dogs, which were thirstily drinking from the stream. The boys were glad there was meat to spare for the dogs. On some hunts the

The Tribe of the Burnt Thigh 91

dogs went hungry because there was only meat for the people. On hunts when no game was found, the starving people ate the dogs.

Soon the smoke from cook fires rose in the air, and the good smell of roasting buffalo made stomachs rumble. The night before, there had been no fires because the band had been passing through enemy land. Supper had been cold parched corn and pemmican—which is what they also ate on the march.

But now they were close to home, where the Ojibwa feared to come.

Still, after all of the food had been eaten, the men of the Guard Society walked through the camp to make sure the fires were doused. They didn't expect the Ojibwa, but a wind rising in the night might scatter hot ashes to flame in the dry grass and leaves.

The women and girls crawled into the small tipis. The men slept under the trees, with weapons ready. The boys snuggled down among the dogs. Soon the camp was still, as the weary people quickly fell asleep.

An owl hooted softly. In a little while, another owl called an answer. Quiet. Then another hoot. It was the signal of the Guard Society that all was well. On nights in the tallgrass land, the signal had been the call of a wakeful meadowlark—a prairie bird.

The owl signal was repeated many times during the night. The watchers of the first guard awakened others to take their places without disturbing the sleeping camp.

Just as the black of the moonless night changed to the gray of beginning dawn, the owl's hoot sounded louder and sharper. Silence followed, but now the guards were alert, eyes moving and searching, nostrils twitching.

The answering hoots came quickly as each guard caught the smoke odor that the first had smelled.

Now the camp stirred. Quietly but quickly, the small tipis became travois and were hitched to the dogs the boys held. The restless animals moved out on a run, with the boys behind them. Following them the women and girls, and the rest of the men all ran to the south.

The little stream of the night's camp was too narrow to stop the leaping flames and too shallow for safety. Trees popped as they burned, and the hot wind carried burning leaves across the water.

The precious meat packs bounced heavily on the women's backs, slowing their flight. The stronger and swifter men took the packs while others grabbed the smaller girls and boys up in their arms.

The boys and dogs led the way toward the deep and wide safety of the Big Sioux River. Before them, and among the fleeing people, ran deer, rabbits, coyotes, mice, and other ground creatures. Hawks, owls, and songbirds flew over and ahead of them.

Coughing and choking, the band ran with tears flowing from smoke-stung eyes. Now the flames were licking their heels. The fire singed moccasins and flared at leggings. Women and girls screamed end beat at their burning skirts.

Into the river plunged the dogs and boys. Others jumped, fell, or were thrown into the water. Steam rose as the flames on burning garments died in the river.

The current caught the swimmers and pulled them downstream. The strong swimmers helped the weaker ones, and soon all climbed or were dragged safely onto the far shore. There they lay, gasping and coughing water and smoke from their lungs. They watched the flames devour the trees and grass on the other side. Wind-borne leaves of fire fell hissing into the water. The fire could not cross the river.

In pain, the people began to move. They walked slowly, limping on bare feet—moccasins and leggings gone. The women's and girls' tunics hung in scorched shreds above their knees.

Late in the day, one of the advance guard wearily waved a robe above his head. The old sentinel of the home village saw the signal and alerted the others to the hunters' return.

The women of the walking band began their shrill vibrating song of greeting broken by wails of pain. The villagers came to welcome the hunters home and filled the air with weeping instead of cheers. They saw that almost all of the men, women, boys, and girls had burnt legs and thighs. The grandmothers ran for their soothing herbs and leaves.

The medicine man moved among the people, giving advice and treating the worst burns himself. After all of the injured had been cared for, the medicine man began to beat his hand drum. His voice rose high in a song that told of the hunting party's run to safety and how good it was that no one had died in the fire.

Over and over, the medicine man repeated the same words and phrases:

> Sicanġu, Sicanġu,
> They return with burnt thighs.
> Sicanġu, Sicanġu.

And to this day, many years after the time of the horse, the descendents of this Lakota band are called Sicanġu, Burnt Thigh.

The White Buffalo Calf Woman

Two hunters were hunting on the plains when a sudden bright light blinded them. They cowered in fear, but the light faded and the hunters saw a beautiful young woman in white buckskin standing before them.

"Don't be afraid," the woman said, and smiled. "Go to your village and tell your people to prepare a council tipi. Soon I will come to them."

Back at the village the people hurried to erect the great council tipi. They waited all night, but it wasn't until the sun rose that the woman came walking in its golden rays. In her hands she bore a bundle. She held it out to the people and walked into the tipi. The people followed.

The woman stood in the center and opened the bundle. "This is the sacred pipe. With it you and all of the people not yet born will send messages to the Great Spirit."

She held the pipe out to the people as she turned in the center of the tipi. "With this pipe walk upon the earth. The earth is your mother and she is sacred. With the pipe all people and creatures on the earth will be joined with the four directions, and with the Great Spirit."

Next the woman taught them how to use the pipe in seven sacred rites.

Then she gave the pipe to the chief. "Remember," she told him, "to always give the pipe respect and honor. Wherever the pipe is, let there be only peace and harmony."

She turned within the circle of the people and left the lodge, walking toward the east. As she went, her white buckskin dress seemed to glow in the sun, and she turned into a white buffalo calf.

The Speck in the Sky

Long ago, in the time when the birds and animals could speak to each other, the birds quarreled. Their voices filled the earth with harsh caws, shrill shrieks, and piercing screams.

The animals, alarmed at the birds' noisy hullabaloo, fled into the thickest forests and deepest caves or climbed to the peaks of the highest mountains. Still, the birds' discordant din was heard everywhere. The animals were furious, and they barked, growled, yipped, snarled, and roared, "Stop!" at the birds. But the birds were so intent on their quarrel that they did not heed the animals' command.

The riotous clamor of the birds and beasts caused the earth to tremble, which frightened the coyotes. They ran yipping down from the hills into the midst of the birds, snarling and snapping until the alarmed birds took flight.

When the birds settled back to the ground, the animals gathered around and sent the great grizzly bear to ask why the birds were quarreling.

This was not the thing to ask, for again the birds began their twittering shrieks as each declared, "I can fly the highest!" and they began arguing again.

"Quiet!" Bear roared and swiped his mighty paws at them.

In the sudden silence that fell over the creatures, the timid voice of Rabbit was heard, "Why don't the birds have a contest?"

"Yes, yes," agreed the animals, "have a contest to decide which bird can fly the highest."

So it was decided. All the birds gathered on a level plain where none sat higher than another. The animals, judges of the race, surrounded the birds.

"Ready?" the bear asked the birds, who lifted their wings.

"Go!"

The air resounded with the drum of beating wings, and the sky darkened as the birds strained upward. At first, the animals, fur ruffling from the tempest of flapping wings, could not tell which bird was the highest. But soon the smallest birds tired and fell behind. Some came down to a gentle landing, while others plopped on the ground. They were followed by the medium-sized birds, who landed with dragging wings and gasped for air with open beaks.

The larger birds still rose in the sky, but soon some began to glide wearily down. Now only those with the most powerful wings soared upward. The animals craned their necks and squinted their eyes to see the tiny forms in the sky.

"How can we tell who's the highest?" the animals wondered, but then there was only one speck in the sky. "Who is it?" they asked.

"It is the eagle," Rabbit answered after checking the birds on the ground.

All the animals cried, "The eagle! Eagle wins!"

Eagle, soaring high above the earth, heard the animals and spread his wings wide, gratefully ceasing his straining flight and beginning a graceful glide back to the ground. Then, as he descended, he felt something move on his back, heard an exultant chirp, and saw a tiny bird fly over his head.

"I win!" the snail bird declared, but soon he began to glide down.

Eagle was too weary to be angry at the little bird and spiraled slowly down to where all the animals and birds cheered his victory.

"I did not win," Eagle said as he landed.

"I did. I won!" chirped the little bird that landed at Eagle's feet.

"How can this be?" wondered the animals and birds. But those feathered beings that were of the same size as the winner wondered most of all because they had been the first to quit.

"How did you do it?" they asked, clustering about the little winner.

"I hid on Eagle's back before the race began," the little one bragged. "Then, when he began to glide to the ground, I flew higher than he!"

Silence fell over the earth as the animals and the birds heard how the little bird had won. Then a low disgusted hum swelled into a disapproving roar of growls and shrieks of "Not fair!" from all the creatures.

None knew what to do until Rabbit timidly suggested, "Let Eagle fly as high as he can, then let the little bird fly as high as he can."

So, a second contest was held. Bear said, "Ready, set," and before he said "Fly!" the little bird was in the air. But even with this head start, the snail bird was back on the ground before the eagle was a speck in the sky.

Until this day, no bird has ever flown higher than the eagle.

Badlands Bones

In the South Dakota Badlands are found large bones of prehistoric animals along with fossils of ancient water creatures. The Indians found these remains long before any white men did, and legends were told about the origin of these mysteries. Legends, although created to explain the unknown, always contain elements of truth, and scientists now know that huge saber-toothed tigers, rhinoceroses, and turtles once lived in the Badlands. They also know that the Badlands were once covered by water.

The Lakota called the area *mako śica,* "bad land," because it was a bad place to travel through. They feared the strange barren formations and the mysterious bones and fossils found there. The following, a retelling of Lakota legends of the Badlands, reflects that fear, but it also tells how good resulted because of the creation of the eagles and the thunderbirds.

*

The Great Sprit had finished forming the earth, but there was still much to be done. He had made mountains and oceans, but the rest was bare. He decided that the land needed rivers and lakes filled with water so that trees and grass would grow on their banks and shores. He took a handful of white clay from the land and fashioned giant men who were strong enough to dig the riverbeds.

The Great Spirit gave the giants a home in the mountain caves they slept in at night. During the day, the giants worked hard digging deep ditches for rivers and deep, wide holes for lakes. As soon as they were large enough, the Great Spirit sent rain that filled them with water. When it rained the giants drank the water and bathed. Then they rested in the mountains.

The giants believed that the water belonged to them because they had dug the river- and lakebeds, so when they found a creature in one of their lakes, they were alarmed.

They didn't know that while they were digging the holes, the Great Spirit had experimented with making creatures to live in water. He made all sizes of fishes and things that had shells, but he had also created a monster. It had a single eye and a long curved horn in the center of its forehead. Red slimy hair hung over its face. It was as big as the giants but twice as long, with an arched back that was almost as tall as a mountain.

Now the giants and the monster looked at each other and were afraid. This was the first time that fear was known on the earth. But curiosity also arrived, and the giants poked and prodded the monster. Now speech came and the giants asked, "What are you?"

But the monster did not understand and did not respond. So one of the giants kicked him, "Why are you in our water?"

But the monster could not speak; it could only roar in irritated fright at being punched, prodded, and kicked. It tried to back into deep water, but as it reared its ugly head to turn, its horn gored one of the giants.

For the first time on earth, blood came from a living creature, and at the sight of it, anger and hate filled the giants' hearts and they threw themselves upon the monster.

The Great Spirit was busy in another part of the earth, but he felt it shake and heard the roars of the monster and the giants as the first mortal battle occurred on the earth's surface.

The Great Spirit quickly rushed to the lake and was alarmed at the great struggle that sent huge waves breaking on the shore. They crashed onto the mountain peaks and emptied the lake.

"Stop!" he commanded, but he was not heard over the giants' shouts and the monster's screams.

The monster's huge head fell into the water, which reddened with blood. The turmoil ceased; the waves ebbed and trickled back into the lake, forming mountain streams.

Now, except for the mud squishing over the dead monster, there was stillness. The giants stood slowly and saw the Great Spirit, but they were not afraid. They had slain the monster and they smiled with vengeful joy.

"You have killed," the Great Spirit mourned.

But the giants had no remorse. They laughed at the Great Spirit and stalked toward the mountains.

"Stop!" commanded the Great Spirit. The giants' laughter made him furious. "Because you have caused death to come to the earth, you can no longer live in my sacred mountains. You will live where your victim died."

The giants shrugged, laughed, and turned to the bloody water.

The monster lay in the drying mud in the deep holes gouged from the lakebed. The mire had formed ragged spires. The crushing waves had washed away parts of mountains and flattened other peaks. What had once been beautiful was now dry and desolate.

"Stay here in these bad lands you have made," the Great Spirit ordered.

So the giants lived in the bad lands.

After that no more rivers or lakes were made, and much of the prairies remained barren. The Great Spirit covered them with grass and placed antelope, deer, and buffalo on the plains.

The giants' anger and disobedience made them hungry, and they fed upon the raw flesh of the dead monster. Again, the Great Spirit was shocked. He sent lightning to make the giants stop, but they caught the lightning bolts and learned to use fire.

After roasting the monster meat, they flung the enormous bones into the bad lands, where they sank in the drying mud.

But now their cooking fires raged out of control, burning the new prairie grass and sending the animals fleeing before the blaze. The giants laughed and raced beside the terrified creatures, catching them up in their hands, and tearing off legs to eat.

Great white eagles, the Great Spirit's sacred birds, flew overhead, but the giants reached up and grabbed them from the air, tearing feathers from wings and tails. They decorated their heads and bodies with the feathers and danced in wild madness. They tossed the eagles into the air, but the missing feathers hindered the birds' flight, and they flew too close to the flames.

Sparks charred spots on some of the eagles' feathers. Others flew to safety on the tall pinnacles in the bad lands. They tucked their heads under their wings to escape the smoke, and all of their feathers were scorched, black, brown, and gray, but their heads remained white and looked as if they were bald. Other eagles came so near the flames that their feathers were singed golden brown.

"Stop!" the Great Spirit thundered at the giants. But just as he spoke, four eagles were struck by lightning. They became thunderbirds who could throw lightning from their talons. When they fanned their wings, winds gusted from four directions and blew down fire. The blaze turned upon itself and died.

The giants were delighted with the turmoil of lightning, thunder, smoke, and fire, and they leapt into the sky trying to catch the thunderbirds.

Now the Great Spirit sent rain and hail to stop the giants, but they lifted their mouths to drink and tossed the ice pellets at the birds.

Harder and faster the rain fell until the bad lands were once more a lake. But the giants climbed to the tops of the highest spires and laughed even as the deluge rose above their knees, to their shoulders, and to their chins. Even when their noses were all that showed, they laughed, and the water bubbled with their mirth. At last the bubbles stopped, and the giants were no more.

The Great Spirit was weary and sad at the destruction of life and land. He rested on a high summit. As he surveyed the flood, he saw the thunderbirds flying in confused circles; they had nowhere to go. They had helped contain the fire, so the Great Spirit gave them the giants' home in the mountains and let them keep the powers of thunder, lightning, and the winds of the four directions.

Soon the lake receded, leaving the land bare. The giants' enormous bones lay where they had been washed by the flood. The Great Spirit sighed and his breath caused the dry earth to rise, and when he stopped, the giants' bones were hidden in the land.

The Flower Nation

The Great Spirit rested after he created the earth's mountains, waters, rocks, and trees. He gazed over his creation and thought, "It is good."

But then he looked more closely. "Something more needs to be done," he mused, as he looked at the green of the trees and grass, the blue of the waters, and the brown and gray cragginess of the mountains.

Slowly the Great Spirit reached out a finger and gently touched the base of a tree and then a sunny spot of grass. Here and there he touched, up the mountain slopes to the peaks and down to curve of the water's edge.

At his gentle touch, his finger left a spot of color. He had created flowers, each different according to its place and all lovely to see.

Pleased, the Great Spirit went on to create animals, birds, fish, and people. He was so busy that he forgot about the flowers.

Soon the first autumn arrived. The animals' fur grew thicker, birds flew to warmer climes, and the people fashioned warm clothing from deerskins and tipis and robes from buffalo hides. The waters formed ice along their edges as the days turned cold. The trees' leaves shivered but were still green.

The earth was preparing for winter — all but the flowers whose blossoms withered in the chill, their leaves curling and shivering in the cold.

The Great Spirit looked again upon his creation, nodding his approval, but his eyes moved restlessly. Something was not right.

Then he saw the faded flowers, their blossoms wilted. "Oh, my children, what is wrong?"

"Father," quavered the flowers, "we are cold, and we are afraid."

The Great Spirit's heart was saddened at the flowers' plight and he pondered what to do for these most beautiful of his creations. His eyes rested upon a tree with shimmering green leaves.

Gently the Great Spirit blew over the leaves on the trees that shook and danced in his wind, and their green turned to vivid red, orange, and gold. "Oh," cried the trees, "how beautiful we are!"

The Great Spirit blew fierce gusts, and the leaves snapped and broke away from the trees. Wildly, the leaves swirled in the wind. "We are flying!" They cried.

Gradually the Great Spirit ceased blowing and the leaves fluttered down to cover the flowers.

The Great Spirit rested again, content. He had created more beauty for the trees, and given the leaves beautiful colors and the joy of flying before they became a blanket for the flowers.

That first winter passed into the first spring. Animals shed their heavy, matted fur; people aired their buffalo robes and lodges. Soon there was new life in nests and tipis as mothers gave birth. The trees' bare branches lifted to the sun; green buds swelled on their limbs and burst into new leaves.

Below the trees, under the dry, dusty blanket, the flowers stirred, poking new growth though the leaves toward the sun and soon blooming.

The Great Sprit walked through the newly awakened earth. "Good," he nodded, but as he looked he saw that during the winter death had claimed some of his creatures.

"Ah," he sighed in sorrow as the spirits of the dead wandered through the spring, confused and homeless. "I could restore life," the Great Spirit thought, "but then the newly born might not have room to grow or enough to eat. I must create another world for the spirits of the dead."

And so he did. A world apart and unseen from the earth. The Great Spirit looked at this world and saw that something was missing. There were trees, mountains, animals, and people but no flowers. He looked back to earth just as the flowers burst into bloom, more plentiful than before.

He gently blew and some of the flowers withered and died. Their fragile, colorful spirits rose into the air. His breath caused clouds to form and rain to fall, and somehow the flowers' dying spirits caught in the raindrops. When the Great Spirit stopped blowing and the sun shone, the yellow flower spirits banded together in an arch over the earth. Soon other flower spirits— reds, blues, and others—followed the golden trail, a glorious glowing rainbow.

The Great Sprit sighed and rested.

All the Time in the World

This tale is an adaptation of two Lakota legends. The first is of the Double Faced Woman. She is the originator of the art of porcupine quillwork. Some fortunate young females dream of this strange woman who imparts her artistic skill to the dreamer.

Quillwork is an ancient art that almost vanished with the introduction of glass beads brought to the tribe by white traders. Women were and are the beadworkers, just as they were the ones who did quillwork. Many traditional quilling designs have been adapted into modern beading. Fortunately, families of quill-workers have passed on the skill through generations of women, so it can still be done today.

The other legend included in this retelling is of an ancient woman who fashions an endless strip of beautiful quillwork and, with her faithful dog, lives forever in the Dakota Badlands.

Deep in the Badlands of Dakota there are many high hills with flat tops. They are called "tables" or "buttes." One of these tables is so isolated that only a few Indians have seen it. But there, so they say, is an ancient woman who, with her dog, has always lived there.

In the tales she is called Old Woman, the grandmother to all of the earth. Her home was a small tipi made from buffalo hides that will never wear out because she cured them with her magic skill.

The tipi's door faces the rising sun whose first beams awaken Old Woman. She rises to begin the many tasks that keep her busy until the sun sets.

Her dog, who is as old as his mistress, is always near her during the day, and at night he sleeps at the tipi's door. However, because of his years, the dog spends most of the day sleeping. But even if his eyes are shut, he is alert to the woman's every move. He flicks his ears and wags his tail whenever she speaks to him or mutters to herself—which she frequently does.

Old Woman also hums and sings as she slowly moves about her chores. The most difficult one—the one that requires the most strength and time—is when she and the dog go for water at the spring near the base of the table. This trek takes most of the morning because her water bag, made from a buffalo stomach, is heavy. Old Woman and Dog frequently pause to rest on the climb up the hill. But there is no reason to hurry, for they have all the time in the world.

But the most important task of the day is not getting the water, vital as it is to the pair's life. This great task can only be done when the sunlight is at its brightest and best for her dimming eyesight. Each day she toils at an intricate design of porcupine quills on an endless strip of soft deerskin. She has quilled the piece ever since time began, and its length lies in a neatly coiled heap. As time passes, it slowly grows.

Old Woman never runs out of quills. She prepared them in her youth long ago, and there is no variation in the colors of the quilled design. Nor does the strip ever have to be pieced with new leather. Old Woman does not question how this can be, nor does she wonder why she must work at the quilling. It is simply a thing she must do.

Once, in the past, she had a dear friend, Double Face Woman. When they were girls together, this friend was the first woman to use porcupine quills in a decorative manner. She taught Old Woman the art before she passed to the spirit world.

Old Woman thinks often of her friend whose double face showed a woman's life. One face was young, happy, and joyful; the other was lined with care and sorrow. This was replicated in the quillwork with colors ranging from gay yellow and red to somber blues and black.

Old Woman also often dreamed of Double Face Woman in the same way that quillworkers—always women—have forever done; for it is in dreams that Double Face Woman imparts her skill to the dreamer.

Each day, after hauling water, Old Woman unrolls a buffalo hide in which the quilled strip is kept and lays it on the ground in front of her tipi. Seated on the robe, Old Woman places her quills within easy reach.

She picks up a quill, puts in her mouth, then pulls it through her teeth. This softens and flattens the quill so that it can be bent and folded into the leather.

Old Woman works industriously for a while, then she stands and stretches to ease the kinks from her aged muscles and joints. She slowly hobbles to add more wood to the fire and tend to her cooking.

The cooking requires her frequent attention during the day,

for Old Woman cooks in the ancient way. She does not have an iron kettle but a buffalo paunch that hangs on a tripod of straight sticks. It is filled with water, dried meat, turnips, and corn.

She places her cook stones in the coals of the fire until they are white hot, then, with a prong of a deer antler, lifts the stones and drops them into the stomach cook-pot. Steam rises as the water bubbles and boils the stew. Cooking this way takes most of the day, so that by the time the meal is ready, the clear light is gone. Soon after she eats, Old Woman goes to bed.

The faithful dog lies near the buffalo robe where the woman quills. He sleeps as she works, but each time Old Woman stands, stretches, and hobbles to the fire, the dog rises, shakes himself, and crawls to the strip of quillwork. He looks to make sure his mistress is tending the fire, then carefully bites the end of the last quill Old Woman put in the design and pulls it loose. Again, he looks to see if his mistress is still busy, and he pulls another quill. When Old Woman is finished at the fire, the dog wags his tail and gives a gentle "woof" of greeting.

Old Woman pats his head and mutters, "šhunka wašte, good dog." Her dim eyes never notice what the dog has done, nor does she wonder why her progress on the quilling is so slow. She believes that she has all the time in the world to finish the beautiful work. Only the dog knows that if Old Woman ever completes her task, time and the world will end.

Glossary with Phonetic Pronunciation

As found in *Dakota English Dictionary* (Ft. Pierre SD: Working Indians Civil Association, 1969) and *Lakota Woonspe Wowapi* (Rosebud SD: Sinte Gleska College Center, 1973).

Akicita (ah-kee-chee-tah): soldier

Dakota, Lakota, Nakota (Dah-koh-tah, Lah-koh-tah, Nah-koh-tah): what the Sioux call ourselves, meaning friends or allies

Han or hanh (huhn): yes

Hau (how): a greeting like hello

Hinh (heenh): an exclamation

Hoka Hey: (ho-kah-hey): a battle cry

Hoksila(s) (hoke-she-lah): boy or boys. Often used as a boy's name

Ina (ee-nah): mother

Kiyuska (key-yoosh-kah): set free

Knikinic (ken-nee-ken-ick): shredded willow bark

Mako sica (mah-koh see-cha): bad land

Santee (sahn-tee): knife, one of the three main divisions of the Sioux

Śha (shaw): red

Śhunka (shoon-kah): dog

Sicanġu (see-canh-joo): burnt thigh, the name of a Lakota band

Takoźa (tah-ko-zha): grandchild

Teton (tee-tahn): dwellers on the plains, one of the three main divisions of the Sioux

Tipi (tee-pee): house or lodge

Tipsila (tip-see-lah): wild turnip

Tiyospaye (tee-yoh-sphey-yeh): extended family

Tunkśi (tuhn-kshee) short for tunkaśila (tuhn-kah-shee-lah): grandfather

Unci (oon-chee): grandmother

Waanatan (wah-nah-tahn): one who charges, or the Charger

Wacintonśni (wah-chin-tohn-shnee): fools

Wakantanka (wah-kanh-tanh-kah): Great Spirit, God

Waśna (wazs-sna): dried chokecherry mixed with suet

Waśte (wash-tay): good

Waśtewin (wash-tay-wee): good woman

Wincincila (wee-chin-chee-lah): little girl

Yankton (yank-ton): campers at the end, one of the three main divisions of the Sioux

Yanktonais (yank-ton-nays): Little Yankton, a subtribe of the Yankton

Acknowledgments

"The Medicine Bag," Virginia Driving Hawk Sneve. *Boys' Life*. North Brunswick NJ: NJ Boy Scouts of America, March 1975.

"The Twelve Moons," Virginia Driving Hawk Sneve. *Tapestry*. Boston: Houghton Mifflin, 1977.

"Clean Hands," *3 Lakota Grandmother Stories: Health Lessons for Young People,* Virginia Driving Hawk Sneve. New York: Association on American Indian Affairs, 1975. Reprinted by permission of the Association on American Indian Affairs.

"The Slim Butte Ghost," Virginia Driving Hawk Sneve. *Houghton Mifflin Reading* by Durr, et al. Copyright © 1986 by Houghton Mifflin Company. Reprinted by permission of Houghton Mifflin Company. All rights reserved.

"Jimmy Yellow Hawk," from *Jimmy Yellow Hawk*, Virginia Driving Hawk Sneve. New York: Holiday House, 1972.

"Grandpa Was a Cowboy and an Indian," Virginia Driving Hawk Sneve. *Image 1*. Glenview IL: Scott Foresman and Co., 1977.

"The First Christmas," Virginia Driving Hawk Sneve. A version of this story first appeared in *Returning the Gift: Poetry and Prose from the First North American Native Writers' Festival,* ed. Joseph Bruchac. Tucson: U Arizona Press, 1999.

"Fool Soldiers," from *Betrayed,* Virginia Driving Hawk Sneve. New York: Holiday House, 1974.

"The Tribe of the Burnt Thigh," Virginia Driving Hawk Sneve. *Houghton Mifflin Reading* by Durr et al. Copyright © 1981 by Houghton Mifflin Company. Reprinted by permission of Houghton Mifflin Company. All rights reserved.

"The White Buffalo Calf Woman," Virginia Driving Hawk Sneve. *On Wings of Peace: Writers and Illustrators Speak Out for Peace, in Memory of Hiroshima and Nagasaki,* ed. Sheila Hamanaka. New York: Clarion Books, 1995.